A SUBTLE DECEIT

Two eligible gentlemen bring Nerissa Cleveland news of her father's death in Egypt — the unassuming Bernard Martin and the darkly abrupt Lord Brook. Both offer to help her to deal with Giles Cleveland's collection of antiquities — which now seems to be at risk from intruders. The neglected house and grounds hold many secrets . . . but who will assist Nerissa in unravelling the mysteries? Does one of her suitors have sinister motives . . . ? And who will gain her love?

Books by Anne Hewland
in the Linford Romance Library:

STOLEN SECRET
TO TRUST A STRANGER

ANNE HEWLAND

A SUBTLE DECEIT

Complete and Unabridged

LINFORD
Leicester

First published in Great Britain in 2008

First Linford Edition
published 2009

British Library CIP Data

Hewland, Anne.
A subtle deceit - - (Linford romance library)
1. Fathers- -Death- - Fiction.
2. Love stories.
3. Large type books.
I. Title II. Series
823.9′2–dc22

ISBN 978–1–84782–676–3

Published by
F. A. Thorpe (Publishing)
Anstey, Leicestershire

Set by Words & Graphics Ltd.
Anstey, Leicestershire
Printed and bound in Great Britain by
T. J. International Ltd., Padstow, Cornwall

This book is printed on acid-free paper

1

Giles Cleveland moved restlessly, only dimly conscious of his weakened body. Someone was here to hold water to his lips and wipe his brow. He no longer knew who it was.

He must be near to death now. At last he would be rejoining his beloved Maria. But what of Nerissa? He had failed their daughter and not only in leaving her a neglected estate and no husband to provide for her. He coughed.

The hot air was rough with flying sand; there was no escaping it. He had come to Egypt to prolong his life and instead lay dying here of a fever. He groaned, thinking of the grey stone walls of Askley, set at the edge of the Dales; how he longed for the fresh, cleansing Yorkshire breezes.

And there was more — worse, much worse than his neglect of his daughter.

He thought, I only wanted to delay the announcement of my discovery. A few weeks — six months at most. I was almost there. And then I could have presented the world with both — the missing pieces of the stone and my solution. It was wrong.

I should have shared it all immediately. I was overly concerned that the new knowledge would fall into French hands and Napoleon's scholars would claim the honour of solving the mystery. Who knows, I might yet have been first. And as it is, because of my greed and folly, my daughter is in danger.

He must take steps to warn her. One last letter while he had the strength. And he must tell her about the key.

He made himself open grit-encrusted eyes to the dark striped fabric of the tent. A strong arm gripped his shoulders, holding a cup to his lips. In one of the rare moments of lucid thought, Giles said, 'Ah, it's you. I should have known.'

'Do not attempt to speak. You must rest.'

Giles struggled to free his right hand from the sheet. 'No — give me paper. I must write.'

His friend did not argue. Efficiently, Giles was supported, a sharpened quill placed between his fingers. The sweat from his shaking hand made the paper damp. Even the first few words were an effort and there was so much he needed to tell her. 'This is for — my daughter. You will find her?'

'Of course. I could write it for you — if you like. What do you wish to say?' He caught the pen as Giles dropped it.

Giles shook his head. The words bubbled in his throat. He thought, I have failed her even in this. Gentle arms lowered him on to the bed as the unfinished note fell to the floor.

* * *

'I am sorry, Miss Cleveland, but your father is dead.'

Nerissa's view of the handsome, smooth-featured face above her was suddenly blurred by tears. The young man was beside her in a moment, taking her arm to steady her. 'I am at fault. Having carried the sad news all this way, I have blurted it out too abruptly.'

'No, indeed. How else could you tell it?'

Lady Hartness was sitting very straight in her chair. 'The news is not unexpected, Mr — Martin, did you say? My brother went out to Egypt ten years ago for his health, a remedy that proved successful for he was at death's door even then, if the doctors were to be believed.'

'You were with my father at the end? You must have been close to him, to be entrusted with this task.'

Mr Martin nodded. 'I would entrust it to no-one else.'

'I am so glad that he had support and friendship at the end. Knowing that helps a little. And you will stay here for a short while, at least? I know you will be eager to return, to continue with your work — that is how my father was though he visited us only occasionally and always in the summer months . . .' Her voice broke. She wanted only to bury her hands in her hair and give way to her grief. But she must stay strong for Lady Hartness. Her aunt seemed to have aged ten years since hearing the news.

'Of course he will stay,' Lady Hartness said.

'But of course — that was always Mr Cleveland's intention,' Mr Martin said. 'I am to be of service to you. May I ask — have the crates arrived before me?'

'Crates?' Nerissa tried to gather her thoughts. 'Yes. There was no word of instruction with them, but that was so like my father. I even thought he might be following in person, to see to their contents, so I have not opened them yet.' She swallowed. How could they be talking so calmly of crates after such devastating news? Yet if she allowed herself to weep, she would never stop.

The intensely blue eyes shared her sorrow. 'And I am sent in his stead. A poor and unworthy replacement, I fear. And I believe that your father wrote during his illness, explaining that I would open them and deal with their contents for you. Hardly a task for a lady.' He smiled.

'Oh, no. You mean to be kind, but I know those are your sentiments and not his. Did my father not tell you? How like him to forget. My passion for Egypt and antiquities is, was, almost as great as his. I had been trying to persuade him to allow me to join him.' She paused. If only she had ignored his strictures. He had been so determined that she must stay in England and secure a husband, as her mother would have wished.

She closed her eyes, remembering the dear face, the last time she had asked him.

'No, child, I should be failing in my duty.'

She should have gone, with or

without his permission. It was not unknown for ladies to make the journey. If she had only been there to nurse him, he might still be alive.

Martin said, 'I will retire, if I may. I would not intrude on your grief.'

'No, not yet. Please. Please tell us everything you can remember. Of his last moments. I have to know.'

As she came to terms with the news over the next few days, it seemed to Nerissa that she had always sensed her father's visit the previous summer would be the last time she would see him. He had seemed distracted and on edge, unlike his usual cheerful self. And he had given her the pendant.

Lady Hartness had been forthright in her disapproval. 'And that has come from someone's tomb? Really, Giles. How can you expect a young lady to wear such a morbid thing? Though better than locked away in that cave of yours which always seems such a waste and not what Maria would have wanted at all.

Her brother had hastened to reassure her — no, this had never graced any tomb, but was in the style of many Egyptian ornaments. 'I have had it made especially.' And more precious to me than an original, Nerissa thought, because of that.

Lady Hartness had not been convinced. 'It is too heavy and ornate with those strange little figures. More suitable for a dowager.' Giles had smiled at his daughter's sparkling eyes. 'They are Apuat, the goddess of the Opening of the Ways,' he said softly, 'and she is paired with Bes, the dwarf god of hearth, home and good fortune. They will bring you their gifts and I hope, remind you of me a little when I am far away.'

Even more so now, with her father buried hastily in a strange land. Because of the fears of contagion, Mr Martin had explained. At least she had the pendant. Nerissa knew it for the most precious object she owned. A memory to be held close to her heart.

Mr Martin proved to be an enthusiastic companion for unpacking Giles Cleveland's crates. A little too enthusiastic at times Nerissa felt, but she could hardly criticise him for that. She too shared in the heady excitement of opening each new box. 'No, no,' she said laughingly. 'I must insist that we work with system and catalogue one crate at a time. My father will have packed with extreme care — linking items together. But of course, you are familiar with his working methods.'

But how refreshing to work with someone in such close companionship. Someone who shared her passion for the beautiful things.

She was not sure how the great idea first took root but it had blossomed as she had woken up one morning. Of course she might still travel to Egypt, to visit her father's grave and continue with his work. Mr Martin could escort her. She frowned. There would be murmuring about chaperones and reputation — would Lady Hartness come too? Had she at last relinquished her hope of finding Nerissa a husband?

But of course! Nerissa sat bolt upright. Why had she not thought of it before? She would marry Mr Martin. How easy — a solution to all her problems. Except that she must now consider how best this may be achieved. Mr Martin might not necessarily consider himself in need of a wife.

Now she regarded Mr Martin in a different light. Over breakfast and during their work with the collection, she considered him surreptitiously. He had a candid, open face with fair hair and blue eyes. Good looks were not of major importance but they were always an advantage and he was pleasing both in face, figure and manner.

'You seem unusually thoughtful this morning,' Lady Hartness said. 'There is something other, I believe, apart from dear Giles' death, that occupies you?'

Nerissa realised that she should have considered this. Her aunt knew her too well. She thought quickly. Far better to achieve her aim with her aunt on her side. In the past, Lady Hartness had proved an invaluable ally in vanquishing one or two suitors Nerissa had viewed with horror — although they might have seemed suitable in other respects, such as wealth and family.

Lady Hartness responded with her usual good sense. 'As you say, suitors have never been great in number. Your dear father's fault, I fear — Askley is too small to be of great value and the estate suffers from the neglect of his absences. It will cost a deal to put right. Mr Martin may well prove the answer and I have already quizzed him on his connections. He agreed that he is a distant branch of the Leicestershire Martins, as I thought he must be. I shall ask him more thoroughly.'

'But if he was my father's trusted friend, that is reason enough to approve him, surely?' Nerissa cried, not liking the sound of this.

'Yes, that speaks volumes for the young man.' Lady Hartness gave a deep sigh of satisfaction. 'It seems that I must wish you joy, my dear.'

'Oh, well — that is, Mr Martin has not yet actually asked me to marry him. Although I am sure he will do so very shortly.'

Lady Hartness laughed. 'I am sure he will if you are determined on it.' She paused. 'You do realise that you will not have two pence to put in your pockets, if Mr Martin has no prospects? My income, small as it is, will die with me; as you know, it comes from my late husband so I cannot help you.'

'That won't matter. We may live very cheaply in Egypt.'

'Not as cheaply as you might think. Living in a tent and enduring hardship is not necessarily cheap. Your father's travels drained the estate even more than your grandfather's extravagances of puzzle and invention.' She paused again. 'Of course, you could sell the collection?'

'No. Never that.' Nerissa did not even need to think about it. 'It was always my father's wish that his collection should be donated to the British Museum. I am even more determined now that there must be rooms there with his name, housing the Cleveland Collection.'

Lady Hartness regarded an intricate stitch in her embroidery. 'Does Mr Martin know this?'

Nerissa raised her brows in surprise. 'He must do. My father will have discussed it with him. He was always talking of it.'

'That is true,' Lady Hartness agreed. She hesitated. 'And are you including the part of the collection that is here already? In the Grotto?'

'Oh. No. I do not feel I wish to part with those — my father kept the Grotto in my mother's memory. It forms the very early part of his collection, which they began together. I do not even know what it contains.' She shook her head. 'Besides, they are at present beyond my reach, until we find the key.'

There was no advantage in delay,

Nerissa thought. Her campaign must be subtle so she must begin at once. It was not so difficult. In spite of her grief, working with Mr Martin in the old steward's room on the ground floor, from the days when the estate had boasted a steward, she was beginning to feel a certain contentment and sense of purpose. This is what her father would have wanted.

Martin was always a pleasant companion. Naturally, one of the maids must always be present but frequently now Lady Hartness herself came to observe the unpacking and cataloguing. 'I wish to observe your strategy, my dear,' she murmured when Mr Martin was out of hearing.

'This is not an entertainment, Aunt.'

'Oh, I think it is. But I know I am old and very dull and seek entertainment in all kinds of unlikely ways.'

Nerissa did not feel she had ever mastered flirting with or without the presence of a chaperone. All the young ladies of her acquaintance during her seasons had seemed to manage it but she could only be direct and felt awkward and uncomfortable. But this must be achieved if she were to succeed. 'I do appreciate your help with this work,' she began, 'when you must be itching to return to Egypt.'

'Not at all,' Mr Martin said. 'The work may seem dull to some but to me it is fascinating.'

She took a deep breath and plunged in. 'In polite convention, I would now pretend to feel slighted and you would say that of course such a companion would make any task seem pleasant.' Nerissa felt herself blushing and peered at the papyrus she was unrolling.

He gave her a startled look. As well he might, Nerissa thought ruefully. I really am not good at this. I am trying to be too clever.

'Oh, I see,' Martin said at last, after an awkward pause. 'I'm sorry, there are few opportunities for gallantry in the Valley of the Kings.'

Nerissa cast around desperately for

what to say next. 'This is nonsense,' she said suddenly. 'I have to tell you. I do value your company and friendship extremely, even beyond your valuable connection with my father. For yourself. If you find me forward, I am sorry but I have to speak as I feel.'

He bowed. 'Thank you. I value such an opinion.'

Quite enough for the present, Nerissa thought. She smiled, flushed with success. He had not seemed to receive her opinion with any kind of dislike. He smiled back. Their hands were almost touching.

'Yes, Wilkins?' Lady Hartness cried suddenly, waking from what seemed to be a convenient doze.

The elderly butler bowed. 'Lord Brook, my lady. I have shown him into the drawing room.'

'Lord Brook?' Lady Hartness put a hand to her throat, her face pale. 'But I thought he was bedridden — in his seventies — no-one expects him to leave his estates in the south.'

Nerissa too was expecting to see the irascible old gentleman who had, when living at nearby Wellsthorpe, proved such a trial to the Cleveland family. She could hardly remember what he looked like. She had been a child when the final rift had occurred between the two families. The boundary between the two estates had been the root of it, she recalled. Old Lord Brook had accused her grandfather of altering the course of the stream to his own advantage.

'By your leave,' a strong voice said as a tall dark presence followed the surprised Wilkins into the room, 'but my news will not wait. Miss Cleveland, I regret to tell you that your father is dead.'

2

Lady Hartness swayed in her chair. Nerissa hurried to support her and glanced over to Martin for assistance. To her surprise she saw that his face also was pale, and with a fixed expression. And there seemed to be something familiar about the stranger although she did not have time to worry about that now. Her throat was tight with anger.

She said, 'I am sorry, Lord Brook, was it? You have the advantage of all of us. And as for the news of my father, I have it already.' She held her aunt's shoulders until Lady Hartness seemed to regain her composure.

Lord Brook frowned. 'So soon? But how can this be? I don't understand. As your father's closest friend, it was his wish that I should be entrusted with this sad duty.'

Nerissa regarded him coolly. The man was obviously some kind of impostor. 'I suppose you will now claim that you were present at his death?' How dare he come here with his lies, to upset everyone? 'How can you suggest such a blatant untruth when Mr Martin is here to disprove everything you say?'

Mr Martin was standing to one side, too well mannered obviously, to intrude in this unpleasantness. But no matter, Nerissa would see that he could hold up his head against this arrogant upstart.

'No,' Lord Brook admitted. 'I was not present, or not aware of the moment of his death at any rate, and to my intense regret. I was struck down with the same fever. But I cared for him as long as I was able.'

Nerissa contented herself with a disbelieving look. And now Mr Martin seemed to have recovered a little. She turned to include him, smiling encouragement. 'Can you vouch for this gentleman's account?'

'Who?' Lord Brook seemed to see the hapless Martin for the first time. 'Who is this? I don't understand.'

'Lord Brook, pray allow me to introduce Mr Martin. Mr Martin brought the news having attended my father at his death.'

'Martin?' Lord Brook muttered. 'I've never seen you before in my life.'

'How can this be?' Nerissa said smoothly, 'when, by your own account, you were both attendant upon Giles Cleveland, my father?'

Martin stepped forward, nodding gravely. 'I do not wish to cause a dispute. It may be that I am not sufficiently memorable — in the havoc caused by the fever epidemic, I may have escaped your notice. Certainly I recall you, sir.'

Lord Brook stared at him for all the world as if he were trying to remember. At last he shrugged. 'No matter. I agree, the camp was in chaos at the time. What matters is my mission here and that the first part of it seems to have been achieved already, if not as I intended. And now, Miss Cleveland, I must perform the remainder and speak with you alone.'

Nerissa was all too aware of poor Martin's relief. And however this Lord Brook had upset Lady Hartness, she too seemed only barely recovered. How dare he? Well, he would find a worthy adversary in her, not so easily intimidated. 'Indeed, you must not. Anything you have to say must be said in front of my aunt.'

Lord Brook inclined his head. 'If you wish. Martin, if you would leave us?'

'No, Mr Martin you must stay where you are. Martin is a very dear and trusted friend.'

'A friend of long standing?'

'That is no concern of yours. This is outrageous.'

'Very well. I merely thought you would prefer a private audience. I have a message from your father. As I said, I but carry out his wishes. His dying wishes.'

She should have expected this, Nerissa supposed. Could she believe him? She did not know what to think. If she did not allow him to pass on the message, even a supposed message, she would always wonder what he had been going to tell her.

'Very well.' She drew herself up in a vain attempt to bring her chin level with his chest. At least she could give an appearance of dignity. 'If you will excuse us, Mr Martin. You may continue here for a while. There is plenty to do still in this first crate.'

'The crates,' Lord Brook said, as if noticing them for the first time. 'They have arrived safely? All seven?' Without waiting for her answer, he began counting silently, nodding at each in turn.

'As you see. And how may that concern you?'

'Why, I dispatched them. Under your father's instruction when he no longer had the strength to see to them himself, which is what he would have preferred, I know.'

'If that is so, you have my thanks.' Nerissa was still regarding him with distrust, looking at him more closely now. There was something familiar about him. She was much more willing to believe that the courteous and quietly spoken Martin had been her father's friend. But what could Lord Brook hope to gain by this charade?

Lady Hartness stood up, her colour fully returned. 'Brook. I must apologise for my foolishness. Your grandfather has died, I presume? We had not heard.' She smiled. 'He and I were very close once. And you are the image of him, as a young man. For a moment I didn't know what to think. What foolishness.' She managed a laugh. 'Yes, I will come with you — to the drawing room? Take my arm, please, Brook.'

Nerissa followed them, feeling suddenly excluded. Her aunt's eyesight was failing, could her instinctive reaction be relied upon?

'Yes,' Lady Hartness was saying, smiling up at Lord Brook. 'With the estates being adjacent, it would have been a happy outcome for all concerned if your grandfather and I could have made a match of it, the difference in our ages was not so great. But it was not to be. He chose elsewhere.'

She turned to speak over her shoulder. 'Eventually he became his grandson's guardian, Nerissa. Surely you recognise our visitor now, my dear? He was your childhood friend — you were inseparable.'

Nerissa felt that she was losing any control of this interview. Was it a mistake to allow Lady Hartness to accompany them, because surely, it couldn't be?

'Edward?' she whispered doubtfully. That must have been at least twelve years ago — and so no more than nine or ten. Surely this was not the boy she had idolised and trailed after, to his constant vexation? She blushed at the thought of it. No, Lady Hartness was seeing and believing what she wished to see and believe.

Nerissa would be less easily convinced. When Lady Hartness sank into a chair, Nerissa remained standing. 'Your message, if you please,' she said briskly. 'Although Mr Martin has already answered all my questions as to my father's last moments, fully and frankly.'

Lord Brook regarded her thoughtfully. 'Ah, yes, Martin. I have to confess, I cannot see where he comes into anything.'

'Forgive me, Lord Brook, assuming you are Lord Brook.' But she knew now that he was her childhood friend, although he was considerably altered. As a youth he had been slim — and diffident in the presence of his grandfather, whereas now he was broad shouldered and strong featured, with a confidence verging on arrogance. She could not approve of his manner and had no intention of making this easy for him. She said, 'I cannot see where you come into anything.'

'I have a note. From your father.'

'A note?' In spite of herself, her breath caught in her throat. 'I already have my father's last letter to me.'

'Ah, yes. There was a longer letter, I know. Written to accompany the crates — and unaccountably lost. There was never time to write another before your father became ill. But he did manage these few words . . . '

'May I see it, please?' Nerissa's heart was beating faster. She did not know what to believe now. Martin had relayed everything so clearly to her; she had been able to picture it all. And now here was the new Lord Brook with his mysterious note.

Surely even he would not lie about such a thing? But once she saw it, she would know, once and for all. She would recognise the well-loved hand.

Her hands were trembling as she reached out for it. She looked at it and gave a small cry of disappointment. The writing was so tortured that she could hardly make it out, let alone recognise her father's hand.

She peered at it closely, mouthing the words as she deciphered them. '*N, there is danger. Ask B —* '

Her feeling of being let down was acute. 'Am I to accept this? And *B* meaning yourself, I presume? How convenient. And what am I to ask you?'

'I don't know. I do not know what he intended to write. However, I do have your father's last verbal request, made to myself in another moment of awareness. This, you need have no further fears or concerns, Miss Cleveland. I will marry you and protect you as your father wished.'

Nerissa stared at him. 'Marry me?'

'Of course. It is the answer to everything.'

Nerissa struggled to find her voice. 'It is not. You come here with this foolish scrawl, playing upon my need to know everything of my father's last moments. How can you think that I would be taken in? And what is this danger? How can there be danger here? It is ridiculous. Even if there were, it is no reason to marry you. I hardly feel I know you.'

For the first time, he smiled. Briefly but the forbidding features were transformed.

'Surely you have not forgotten how I came here as a boy, fascinated by your father and his talk of Egypt. I trailed after him and you trailed after me.'

'You must remember,' Lady Hartness chimed in. 'You were well nigh inseparable.'

'That was a long time ago,' Nerissa said stiffly. 'And you bear little resemblance to the boy I remember.' Shy, eager, only too willing to escape his tyrannical grandfather.

As a foolish child, yes, she had idolised him. 'However, I cannot see how that has any relevance now.'

He was frowning again. 'You would not gainsay your father's wish? When I was only too willing to fulfil his request?'

'I trusted my father's judgement implicitly. But I only have your word for this. Even your note does not bear you out. You are completely at variance with everything Mr Martin has told me. And I have quickly grown to know and trust him. In fact — ' No. She made herself clamp her lips together tightly.

She had almost blurted out that she was to marry Martin — and before he even knew of it. Disastrous. But that was the effect this overbearing man was having upon her.

'If you will not take notice of me, surely you will regard the note? You must appreciate that there is danger and heed your father's warning. My presence as your husband will safeguard you and your household.'

Nerissa did not trust herself to speak. She contented herself with a haughty glare.

'Lady Hartness,' Lord Brook said. 'May I appeal to you? I am at fault here. I should obviously have approached you first.'

'To advance your suit with my niece? Yes, maybe you should.'

'Aunt! There will be no further talk of suits. No, Lord Brook, I can give you my answer at once. I will not marry you. I can think of nothing that would be further from my wishes. And now, if you will excuse me, I have to proceed with my work. Here at least, I am certain of what my father wanted.'

She left the room and strode along the corridor, clenching her nails into her palms. How dare he! The presumption, the arrogance. Coming here with this nonsensical tale and expecting her to fall into his arms, overwhelmed with gratitude.

Now more than ever, she needed the calming effect of her father's collection. She paused outside the steward's room, breathing deeply. She would have loved to confide in Martin, but commonsense told her that this would not be a good idea.

If Martin had a fault, it was that he lacked confidence in himself and was not always willing to push himself forward when he might. Indeed if he knew that Lord Brook had declared himself, Martin might well withdraw from the marriage contest before ever realising he was a part of it.

Nerissa shook her head. No, that was nonsense. But she must consider carefully how best to approach the matter afresh. Lord Brook had thrown her plans for a leisurely courtship into disarray. Odious man. Well, let Lady Hartness deal with him and send him away. She had no intention of facing him again. She opened the door.

For a moment she did not see Martin. He was in the far corner of the room, amongst the crates they had not yet tackled. He looked up in surprise. 'Is everything all right? Your visitor did not stay long. I was trying to think how I might remind him of my presence in the camp.'

Nerissa dismissed Lord Brook with an airy wave of the hand. 'Oh, do not worry about him. I did not take any account of his wild stories. My aunt will send him packing. I have heard all I wish from him. More than enough. I just wanted a few moments with the figures here, to recover myself.'

She gazed at them fondly, picked one up and smoothed the ancient surface. 'They are so timeless. What have they seen with these painted eyes?' She replaced it with care. 'They are all that matters to me at present. I am not going to allow anyone, least of all Lord Brook with his prattling of unspecified perils, to distract us. The sooner I have fulfilled my father's aims and presented the collection to the British Museum, the sooner I shall be satisfied.'

'The British Museum?' Martin murmured. For a moment his eyes held a look she could not read.

'Yes, did I not mention it? Surely my father will have told you? At times he would speak of nothing else.' She explained her father's vision. 'The Cleveland Collection. That sounds very grand, does it not? And a lasting and worthy monument.'

'Yes, indeed.' Now he was speaking

with enthusiasm. 'A memorial to your father's name. But how soon will this occur? Are you to continue with the cataloguing? If it is proving too onerous for you, I can continue alone.'

Nerissa laughed. 'Oh, no. I enjoy it. And I would never allow the museum to take over too soon, denying myself all the fun. No, I have not even approached them yet. I would deprive neither of us of this pleasure.'

She smiled, feeling almost her usual self again although poor Martin still seemed on edge. And no wonder. Lord Brook would be enough to unsettle anyone.

She said gently, 'Truly, it is your account of my father's death that rings true to me. Lord Brook's behaviour is only to be expected — the family have always been erratic. Which is why my grandfather quarrelled with old Lord Brook I believe. Though again, my grandfather was also a man of strange whims and fancies.

'This house and grounds are a

monument to his quaint predilection for inventiveness. Secret openings, hidden passages, doorways disguised as panelling and panels that look like doors — subtle deceits of every kind. I must show you some of them some time. They have been sadly neglected of late and may not work so well. I loved them as a child. And you will hardly believe that Lord Brook, who was so ill mannered to you just now, used to come and play here and loved them too. That was before the family quarrel of course.'

She was speaking at random and noted with pleasure that the idle words were having their effect in restoring Martin. Already he seemed more settled and the colour had returned to his face.

By the time Lady Hartness returned, they were working away as if nothing had happened. 'Oh, I should have called for Betty,' Nerissa said cheerfully. 'I forgot. I presume Lord Brook has left?'

'For the moment.' Lady Hartness

had a strange expression and a twinkle in the grey eyes. 'I am afraid I had no alternative, my dear, when Lord Brook had explained his position. His aim in returning here following the death of his grandfather is to restore and refurbish Wellsthorpe but as we all know, the place is presently uninhabitable — particularly after the fire and the storm last winter.'

'Yes?' Nerissa spoke with foreboding. 'Aunt, what have you done?'

Lady Hartness continued blandly, 'I could see no alternative but to offer our hospitality. He is to stay here while the repairs are carried out.'

3

On the following morning, Nerissa took care to greet Lord Brook, his man and his luggage in person. Evidently Lady Hartness still held a romantic tenderness for his late grandfather, which had clouded her judgement. Nerissa said, with a cool smile, 'So we are to enjoy the pleasure of your company after all? Well, you may have insinuated yourself with my aunt, but do not think to do the same with me.'

Lord Brook managed to look pleased with himself even without smiling. 'I can only apologise for the difficulties of our meeting. I was taken aback when I had thought to be the first with the tragic news — I had expected to be called upon to support you in your grief and was put at a disadvantage.'

Nerissa found herself warming to the sentiment, so frankly expressed. 'I can see that it might,' she said cautiously.

'But try as I may, I still cannot recall Martin, which troubles me. The camp was never large, although as the fever took hold, necessarily we had to employ numbers of Egyptian bearers and servants unknown to us. Those who would risk the infection in return for more money. As I said, that might account for his presence — particularly if he found himself rootless and unemployed.'

'We will not discuss Mr Martin behind his back if you please. Only when he is present and able to defend himself.'

'Also at that time, I was almost wholly concerned with caring for Giles. I hardly left the tent. If Martin arrived then, it would be understandable that I did not meet him. But now I am here, I will have plenty of time to ask him. Will he be staying long?'

'He is a fellow guest,' Nerissa cried. 'I will not have you browbeating him about this. He had proved himself loyal and true to my father, has brought me the most caring letter, has given me little details of his last days . . . ' Her voice broke. 'While you have shown me only a dishevelled paper which could have been written by anyone.'

Lord Brook stiffened. 'How can you doubt me? This is incredible. I am only interested in the truth.'

'The truth is that my father is dead, and that at the last Bernard Martin cared for him. And quite possibly you were there at the same time. No, Lord Brook, I do not wish to discuss this further. I do not wish Martin's precious account to be marred by petty argument. It is all I have.'

'Very well.' Lord Brook bowed.

Nerissa breathed deeply. What was she thinking of? Brook's boorishness was no excuse for greeting a guest in this way. 'We have given you the Red Room, I believe.' Although faded now to a dusty pink. But it could not be helped. He would have to accept the housekeeping as he found it — along with the creaking floorboards and doors, which either swung loose in the slightest breeze or could not be opened without a sharp push.

He to seemed to be making an attempt at civility. 'Ah, I remember. I can continue my search from there. As children, we spent hours searching for the secret spy holes and cupboards that were your grandfather's legacy.'

'Or you did. You were very solemn about it. I trailed after you, getting in the way.'

'Did I say that?'

'Once or twice.'

He laughed and for a moment was different again. 'Then I must apologise once more.' He shook his head. 'But although I spoke in haste yesterday and truly regret my lack of manners, I must emphasise the danger you are in while the collection remains here. Even with myself here to protect you.'

And just as she had been softening towards him a little. 'I thought you were here because your own house was uninhabitable? But no matter. I must repeat — there is no danger. We are quiet here, in the tranquillity of the Yorkshire countryside. We have only Bailford and the Royal Oak where we may look for diversion; fashionable society avoids us. There are no wealthy society ladies who might possess the riches and jewellery to tempt thieves.'

'Your father's discoveries present a tempting target,' he murmured under his breath. 'Not to mention the notes about his work.'

She had no intention of discussing her father's work. If Lord Brook were seeking information, he would be disappointed. 'A target for whom? Come, Lord Brook, am I to believe that an army of Egyptian pashas and mamelukes is to sweep across the park at any moment?'

'Brook, Brook, you are here,' Lady Hartness cried, entering the room in haste. 'How welcome you are. Nerissa is right, we are sadly quiet here. But Brook, you cannot tell me that Giles' motley collection of quaint little figures and bric-a-brac is in any way valuable?'

Nerissa gave him a warning glance. How much had her aunt heard? She particularly did not wish the older lady to be alarmed by Brook's fanciful fears. 'No, of course it is not. My father was more interested in the strange and unusual rather than the gold or gems that tempted the tomb robbers.'

'So — ' Lord Brook seemed to struggle for his reply and then, to Nerissa's relief, changed the subject. 'How are you attempting the classification? Are the items to be placed on display, as they deserve?'

Nerissa thought quickly. Was he going to offer his help? If so, and he lacked the expertise he claimed, his imposture would be revealed all the more quickly. Although she would regret the loss of her friendly sessions with Martin — and must think of some other way to further her pursuit of him. But she could hardly refuse Lord Brook in this.

‘As to the classification — ’ She explained how the articles were being arranged on the shelves. ‘So far it has not been at all difficult. The first crate at least has been packed intelligently.’

He shrugged. ‘Of course. By myself, after discussions with Giles. But they are to remain in that room, where I saw them? So near the rear doors and overlooking the stable yard?’

‘You seem to have noticed a great deal in the few minutes you were there.’

‘Naturally, because their safety is important. And you forget, I am familiar with every corner of your house. Could they not be moved to where they will be displayed permanently? Surely that will be more secure?’

Nerissa hesitated. She explained again how the bulk of the collection was destined for the British Museum. ‘But I am beginning to feel that I would like to keep some pieces for myself. That will not be difficult to arrange for many are in duplicate. And these could ideally be displayed with the items brought from earlier expeditions.'

She paused. Now was the opportunity for Lord Brook to prove his recent connection with Giles Cleveland. He said nothing. She continued, 'In the Grotto? In the grounds?'

'Ah, yes. I remember. And before the stream changed its course, those caves belonged to Wellsthorpe.' He spoke without resentment. 'And the Grotto is secure?'

'Perhaps you may advise me here. All too secure, I am afraid. It is locked and I do not have the key. You have not brought it with you? Accompanying your 'note'?'

Brook frowned. 'I am afraid not. But I assume then that Martin was not entrusted with it either?'

'There could be any number of explanations,' Nerissa said quickly. 'My task is to discover it somehow. It may have been here all the time.' She bit her lips, fearing she had said too much. But Lord Brook was returning to his original theme.

'I am aware of the regrettable lack of able-bodied servants here. No, I must speak of this. Giles and I often spoke frankly round the flames of the evening campfires and I am aware of your financial circumstances. If I could enlist some of my own men, to patrol the grounds at night, perhaps guarding the stable yard — or even within the house, my mind would be easier.'

Nerissa made every effort to keep her temper. 'Lord Brook, I do not believe you are listening to me. You persist in continuing with your own thoughts and theories as if I had said nothing. I will hear no more of this. Please put all your efforts into ensuring that your own house is repaired with the utmost speed. I do not wish to be ill mannered and I hope that your stay with us will be as comfortable and as pleasant as it may be, for all of us. But we will all be most happily served if your stay is as brief as possible.'

He bowed again. 'I shall attempt to fulfil all your requirements.'

'And now if you excuse me? I will leave you to settle in.'

* * *

Nerissa had thought herself weary when she finally retired that evening after a day fraught with discord and conflicting emotion at every turn. As soon as her head touched the pillow, however, her thoughts set up a clamour that would not be denied. Why did Lord Brook make her feel so uneasy? Why make that ridiculous proposal of marriage, which had not been mentioned again? Was he seeking to gain control of the collection by marrying her? If so, he had failed.

And all those prying remarks about her financial circumstances and the able-bodied servants? No, it was not only her financial situation that he was all too knowledgeable about. She would not, could not trust him, his story did not hang together properly. She must be on her guard, might even share her suspicions with Martin and enlist his aid.

Thank goodness Mr Martin had arrived first — otherwise she might have fallen into the trap of believing Lord Brook. She did not even have to seek too far to discover his motivation, considering the bitterness that had arisen between the two families. In marrying her, he would have regained the stream and the disputed land. If he had met and spoken with her father, this might be a part of the whole, all in order to regain what he felt he had lost.

Fortunately she had outwitted him. A pity Lady Hartness had trustingly allowed him to stay, but it could not be helped. She had the advantage; he did not know she suspected him.

If only she had the key she thought as she drifted into sleep. But then her father had been thoroughly a Cleveland, as was she — he would have made a suitable provision for the key and the answer would not be straightforward. Why had she not thought of that before? The key would be concealed somehow with a puzzle to solve. She must make certain that she solved it before Lord Brook. She was smiling as she slept at last.

Only moments later it seemed, she awoke abruptly. Her heart was beating rapidly as she sat up, staring into the darkness.

Somewhere downstairs she could hear shouting and doors banging. Even the crash of breaking glass. She felt for her wrap and groped her way to the landing, without a thought for any possible threat to herself. Lord Brook had been right. The collection was in danger.

4

In the flickering candlelight, the landing seemed to be filled with figures. Lady Hartness with a pair of fire irons, Martin with flushed face and tousled hair. 'Ladies, please return to your rooms. I will see what's happening.'

'And be murdered in our beds?' Lady Hartness cried. 'I think not. I prefer to face my adversary.'

Nerissa peered over the banister rail. 'Who is downstairs?' Very persistent intruders it seemed, as the noises from the steward's room showed no sign of abating. How dare they, whoever they were? Inspired by a further sweep of anger, she set off down the stairs.

A familiar figure and voice from below. 'No, Lord Brook, please be silent. You will wake the house.'

She called out in relief, 'Wilkins! Are you all right?'

'There, I knew it.' The old man's voice was trembling with distress. 'Pray, do not alarm yourselves. All is in hand. All is safe.'

Nerissa ran down the stairs, careless of tripping. 'So what is Lord Brook doing? Is he attacking someone? Martin, come down and help him.'

But here was Lord Brook in person, dishevelled but unharmed. 'Wilkins is right, they are gone.' He seemed better prepared for the emergency than anyone else did, as he was fully dressed. 'No sign of anyone in the yard. There's the broken window of course but Wilkins and I will easily see to that straightaway.' He seemed to be alight with enthusiasm as if enjoying some boyish adventure.

'Please begin at the beginning and tell us what happened.' Nerissa glared at him.

'I heard a noise, I am a light sleeper in a strange bed, and I came down. I believe I must have disturbed an intruder. Or intruders.'

'More than one?' Lady Hartness exclaimed.

Brook flung wide the door with a dramatic gesture, inviting them to step inside. Two of the windowpanes were broken and the frame swung open, the hasp bobbing gently, scraping the frame as the breeze caught it.

Nerissa stifled a gasp, a hand to her throat. She must set an example of calm to the household and avoid female tremors but the shock of the sight had affected her deeply. The empty crate tipped on its side, some small vases on the shelf knocked over while a jackal-headed statuette lay on the floor at her feet. She stopped to pick it up, unable to assess the damage through a blurring of tears.

'The glass . . . take care . . . ' Lord Brook said helpfully. 'Your feet . . . '

Nerissa glanced down but saw no shards of glass catching the candle flame. Most of them must have fallen outside. 'Not easy to tell but everything seems to be here. I think you must have disturbed the robbers just in time, Lord Brook. I owe you my thanks.'

Wilkins pulled the window closed and secured the hasp. 'There are only a couple of panes broken. We can repair it easily enough.' His voice was faltering. She knew that the attempted robbery had upset him deeply.

Martin was suddenly at her shoulder, now also fully dressed. 'Perhaps it would be best if the ladies returned to their rooms now. Might I volunteer to check everything thoroughly?'

'I think that could wait until morning,' Nerissa said. She wanted to perform that task herself but was aware of a wave of weariness.

'I also feel that a watch should be kept. Someone should stay here and keep watch for the rest of the night. I wish to volunteer my services.'

'And I too,' Lord Brook said quickly.

'Thank you, Mr Martin. An admirable idea. And one watcher will be quite enough, I am sure. You have been kept from your rest long enough, Lord Brook.'

'It doesn't matter. Not compared to your safety.'

'We are safe. Mr Martin has volunteered. And you need your sleep if you are to begin your labours in the morning as planned, giving the work at Wellsthorpe your full attention. I insist on it.' They glared at each other, eyes locked as if no one else might be present.

Nerissa knew she sounded waspish and irritable; but the strain of arising abruptly from sleep and the shock of the discovery were taking their toll. This would happen during Cobham's night off — if present he could have given warning from his quarters in the stables.

'I bow to your determination,' Lord Brook said.

Nerissa breathed a sigh of relief. 'Wilkins will bring you anything you need, Mr Martin. More candles, refreshments, is there anything else?'

'No, thank you. I was accustomed to snatching sleep when and where I could in Egypt. As you say, Lord Brook has played his part in discovering the danger and I must make my contribution.'

Nerissa smiled warmly at him. She lifted her hand to press his arm encouragingly and thought better of it as she saw that Lord Brook was regarding her with what might have been a look of mockery. 'I am grateful for your support, Mr Martin.' She placed an arm around her aunt, ready to usher her up the stairs. 'Lord Brook?'

He was staring intently around the room. 'Yes, we may examine the collection more carefully by daylight.'

'Certainly.' To her relief he made no further argument but meekly ascended the stairs behind them. Nerissa made a pretence of helping her aunt, observing him from the corner of her eye. 'Child, I am not in my dotage,' her aunt protested.

'Of course not. You will remember to prop your door closed? I think a wind is getting up.'

'Yes, indeed, I have my pile of old books at the ready. And if anyone should try anything with me, I shall use them as missiles, do not fear. Young Jack Bartlett is fashioning a most handsome doorstop for me and when that is finished, it will make an even better weapon.'

Nerissa smiled. 'I hardly think that will be necessary.' At last the door of the red room creaked shut behind Lord Brook and Nerissa felt that she could relax a little. I would be better at keeping watch, Nerissa thought for I can recognise every squeak of the woodwork and the distinctive sound of each door. I would soon identify any untoward night-time ramblings. She could not feel entirely happy about Lord Brook's discovery but was not sure why.

If I lie awake for a while, I will know what's happening, she told herself. She lay there, hoping that Wilkins had obeyed her and had returned to his bed. A system of night-time watches might well be a good idea, but how might she prevent Wilkins from volunteering? She could not give her true reason for his feelings would be greatly hurt if he felt she considered him too old for the duty.

Surely however, they would not need these precautions for too long. The attack must have been performed by some passing opportunist — an injured infantryman maybe, discharged and penniless, who deserved their pity. Now that it was obvious that Askley held nothing of value, the attack would not be repeated. Discouraged by Lord Brook, the intruders would be far away by now and seeking easier pickings.

In spite of her intention to stay awake as long as possible, she was next opening her eyes to first light. She lay tense and still, knowing that something had awoken her again. The telltale creak of Lord Brook's door? She could not hear anything now. She sat up carefully. Something was wrong.

Yes. Outside, the door of the red

room groaned softly as if someone was trying to conceal the sound. What was Lord Brook doing now?

No matter that her own door betrayed her presence as she pushed it open; she wanted to catch him. He was at the top of the stairs, peering downwards.

'I heard something,' Nerissa said.

'So did I.' He put a finger to his lips. Whatever they had heard, the whole house was now silent. He murmured, 'I am going to check the room.'

'I will come with you.'

'No. If anything untoward has happened . . . Stay here.' He went silently down the stairs without troubling to ensure that Nerissa was obeying him. She did not. As soon as he reached the hall, she set off behind him. 'Does he think I might have an attack of the vapours?' she murmured furiously to herself. 'And what if he should be attacked in his turn? Where should we be then?'

When Lord Brook reached the

doorway of the steward's room, Nerissa was only a dozen paces behind him, to hear his cry of, 'Martin, good grief, man!'

Her heart thumping, Nerissa raised the hem of her nightgown in her hands and hurried along the corridor. 'They have come back,' she cried.

'So it would seem.' Lord Brook was kneeling beside Martin who was lying on the floor amidst a wreckage of straw and broken pottery. The younger man's face was covered in blood.

Hand to her mouth, Nerissa cried, 'Martin. Oh, no.' At least he was struggling to rise. 'Keep still,' she said briskly, ashamed of showing her terror. 'I will fetch some water.'

'No,' Lord Brook said. 'You are safer here. I will get it.'

'There is no need,' Martin's voice was weak. 'Nothing but a graze. Let me come with you, Brook. My assailants may still be within the house.'

'I was hoping to avoid pointing that out,' Brook said sharply. 'Keep still, man, while Miss Cleveland tends you. No heroics, if you please.'

Nerissa sighed her relief as he left the room. 'Are you able to tell me what happened?' She didn't wish to bombard him with questions as yet — but he was right about the continuing danger. And better a gentle interrogation from her than a fierce barrage of demands from Lord Brook.

Martin put a hand to his forehead, wincing visibly at the sight of the blood on his fingers. 'The collection . . . in ruins. Oh, Miss Cleveland, can you ever forgive me? I have let you down badly. And your father.'

'No need to speak of forgiveness. It was hardly your fault.'

'You see, my watch began quietly enough. I seated myself to face the window, reasoning that any further attack would come from the same direction.'

'Of course. I understand.'

'And then, there was a sudden rush of movement behind me. And I felt a blow to my head and knew no more.

Not until I heard Lord Brook's voice.' He paused. 'Strange is it not, that he should be first on the scene? No, take no notice. I am rambling. It is the blow on the head.'

'He may have disturbed them again.' Nerissa shivered. Maybe Lord Brook was indeed a very light sleeper. She went to a cupboard where clean dusters were always kept in readiness, to use on the Egyptian items.

'Oh, I think they will have completed their task,' Martin said bitterly, 'with myself useless to stop them. I have betrayed your trust. Look at this mess.'

'No collection, however rare, can justify the risk of life and limb,' Nerissa said. 'We must have no more of it.'

'A little dramatic,' Lord Brook said as he re-entered the room. 'Merely a graze, Martin.' He set down a jug and a bowl and more clean cloths. Obviously he had found his way around the kitchen.

'Only by great good fortune.' Nerissa's eyes flashed in anger. 'He could have been killed.' How could Lord Brook be so heartless?

'Did you see your assailant?' Lord Brook demanded.

'Lord Brook, please. Not now.' Nerissa dabbed at the oozing blood. It did look worse than it was. Lord Brook had been right in that. But it was bad enough and must be painful.

Martin groaned. 'No, I can speak. Indeed I must.' He repeated what he had told her.

'Is that all?'

'I don't know, let me think a moment. All was darkness after the blow and then, yes, I came to my senses a little and realised they were still here, moving around — I believe one of them said something. It might have been, 'Have you found anything?' And next thing, Lord Brook's voice on the stairs. They must have taken to their heels, I don't know. I lost consciousness once more. Briefly.'

'So you must have gained some impression of them. Were they tall, thickset? Young, old?'

Martin shook his head and winced with pain. 'I can't say.'

'What were their voices like?' Lord Brook sounded impatient. 'Deep? Rough? Did they speak in the Yorkshire dialect?'

'No, I can't remember.'

'At least you can surely tell me what answer was made to the question.'

'Question? I don't understand.'

'You stated that one asked the other if he had found anything? Had he? What was the reply?'

'I don't recall a reply. I am doing my best.'

'Mr Martin has been through an ordeal that would tax anyone. He needs to rest, quietly. And then maybe he may remember more. But I for one am exceedingly grateful that he has answered your questions as fully as he has. Without him being here, who knows what might have happened? No, keep still, Mr Martin. I am almost done.' She sat back on her heels as a thought struck her. 'Besides, Lord Brook, I can't believe that you didn't see them.'

Lord Brook shrugged. 'I can hardly believe it myself.'

Nerissa bent again to her task. He must have seen them. He had been looking down at the hall as she left her room. Could she trust anything he said? Strange too, when he had been so fortunately vigilant earlier in the evening that he should come upon the scene so late. A cold shiver flashed down her spine. Might he be in league with the intruders?

'Thank you, Miss Cleveland,' Martin said earnestly. 'I feel able to continue with my watch now — if you will entrust me with the task.'

Nerissa and Brook exclaimed against this together. 'Indeed you will not. You must sleep now.'

'You are not fit for anything, man. See, here is Wilkins. He will take you upstairs and I will continue the watch.'

But the old man was wringing his hands in agitation. 'That this should happen again. And I am certain that I checked the rear door before retiring. It was locked and bolted as always. I can't understand it.'

Lord Brook nodded. 'Yet as I went to the kitchen, it was wide open.'

'So that is how they got in,' Martin said.

'Or out,' Lord Brook added. 'Don't worry, Wilkins, they might have got in some other way and unlocked the door to leave themselves a way of escape.'

Nerissa's thoughts were whirling. There had been all the bustle and commotion of the earlier warning that night. Could the door have been overlooked? Or might someone have left it open purposely once Wilkins had checked it? Would Lord Brook have had such an opportunity?

'I believe we must have two people on watch at all times,' she said firmly. 'Wilkins, if you would watch until morning with Lord Brook?' A risk she must take. Surely Brook would not attack an old man? And shortly the rest of the servants would be awake. This watch would be very brief.

Brook said, 'We are assuming that they have left, and we do not know how they got in. If you would accompany me, Wilkins, we should check all the ground floor rooms and all the doors and windows before anything else.' There was a note of concern in his voice.

Nerissa glanced at him and in the increasing light of dawn, saw a troubled frown on his face. 'If we could arouse the other male servants, because some-one must stay here with Miss Cleveland. And Martin. In fact, I am surprised they have not appeared.'

'That is because there aren't any.' Nerissa said briskly. 'Only Cobham in the stables and I believe it is his night off and Jack Bartlett, the boy who cares for the gardens and lives with his grandmother.'

'I'm sorry for that,' Lord Brook said quietly. 'I had not realised the situation to be so acute.'

No, because Nerissa had done her best to resist telling him. Well, he knew now and she wished he did not. But there had been no way to avoid his finding out, now he was staying here. If only Lady Hartness had not fallen so swiftly for his plausible story.

She must find out what he wanted, Nerissa thought as she went back to her room once again. If he had packed the crates as he claimed, he must know what they contained. If her father had already been ill, could Lord Brook not have stolen what he wanted at that time? And what could it be?

She must observe him at all times and seek to catch him out. At least he had as yet no idea that she suspected him.

5

Lord Brook's watch was not spent quietly however. Nerissa came downstairs to the sound of hammering. What could be happening now? She burst into the steward's room to be met with a very different scene of confusion. All the crates were stacked neatly against the rear wall, two men she did not recognise were working on the window and Lord Brook, in his shirt sleeves, was unpacking panes of glass from shavings and straw.

'Ah, Miss Cleveland, as I thought. These will do admirably. I had them cut for some of my own windows but your need is greater and they fit perfectly.'

'But, I didn't authorise this.'

'There was no need to trouble you. I hoped you would rise later and I would have it all in place. You have caught me out.' He grinned.

'Thank you.' What else could she say? But she did not wish to be beholden to him. And watching him closely had proved impossible already. 'I thought I made myself clear. I wanted to examine the collection myself, to see what was missing.'

'And you still can. See, everything that was on the floor has been placed in this empty crate and I have merely straightened the items on the shelves. There is nothing else damaged. We are lucky in that. Ah, I fear we are in the way here.' He laughed.

'Come out into the yard and I will demonstrate how we have strengthened the frame.'

'Yes, we seem to be,' Nerissa murmured. How dare he tell her she was in the way, in her own house, even if it was true. But his pleasure in the task was infectious. He was like a young hound, she thought, at his happiest when he had something to do. She followed him into the stable yard. Slivers of glass on the cobbles caught and reflected the morning sunlight.

Lord Brook was explaining that they could install new shutters, to be closed and locked securely. Nerissa stared down at the glass. Something was troubling her and she didn't know what it was.

'And my workmen can stay on and help with the watches,' Lord Brook said cheerfully.

'I beg your pardon? Oh, no. No, indeed. Your house — I mean, they are needed there. Their absence will disrupt your repairs. I couldn't ask it of you.' His return would be delayed still further. She tried to conceal her horror. And Lord Brook's men would be answerable only to him and equally untrustworthy.

'Then I shall hire more men.'

'I do not wish you to do so.'

'They need the work. This is providing employment for men with families. There has been a shortage of gainful labour here since my grandfather allowed the estate to fall into neglect. I have a great deal to make up.'

Nerissa knew she had lost. He had hit on the one argument she could not oppose. If only she had the resources to rebuild Askley and provide work for the villagers, some of whom had been loyal to the Clevelands for centuries. The area needed Lord Brook and his inherited wealth. 'Very well. That is an aim I admire.'

Lord Brook beamed at her. 'That is excellent. And there is something else I need to ask. I must prevail upon your kindness once more I fear.'

'Yes?'

'I am expecting guests at Wellsthorpe. I gave the invitation before realising the state of the house. Foolish, I know. But now, I am in a dilemma.'

Nerissa could not imagine anything more unlikely. Lord Brook was hardly the kind of man to behave so thoughtlessly. No, everything he did and said was with a definite purpose. 'Yes?' She found herself curious as to what he was going to say next. Who could they be? She could hardly welcome his guests. They would inevitably be part of his plot. But she could not for the moment see how this could be avoided.

'Two only. If they might stay here instead, we should all be most grateful to you,' Lord Brook said eagerly, obviously delighted by the prospect of getting his own way. 'They are my oldest friends. Mr and Miss Northcott? Brother and sister. I have known Northcott since my schooldays. There was always a welcome for me at their home, Woodleigh, during the holidays when there would be none with my grandfather. He made it plain, after the rift with your family occurred, that he wished nothing further to do with me.' His face was dark.

Nerissa could not prevent a wave of sympathy mixed with anger on behalf of that poor boy. But perhaps this was Lord Brook's intention? She must be on her guard. Although surely a Miss Northcott would not be involved in

Brook's plot, whatever it might be? Why bring her here? Perhaps I am imagining the whole thing, Nerissa thought.

'And Mr Northcott could be of great assistance with the collection. He has worked with the British Museum and will be able to help. Particularly with the security issue.'

This was the last thing Nerissa had been expecting. 'But I told you, I'm not ready to make contact with the museum.'

'Mr Northcott will not interfere with our, with your, way of doing things, I can assure you. And it seems that events are forcing our hand. We must do something or risk losing the collection entirely. The risk is too great.'

He was right of course. But she could not relish the thought of the unknown Miss Northcott turning up her nose at the household arrangements — or lack of them. 'We are very simple here, I do not think Askley is suitable for a lady guest.'

Lord Brook grinned, 'Oh, Sophie

won't mind. She can take anything and still keep a good humour.'

Nerissa felt an unexpected twinge, somewhere in the region of her heart. She didn't know why. Was it the easy, friendly way he had referred to this Sophie? But why should that matter? Lord Brook and his friendships meant nothing to her. Annoyed with herself, she shuffled pieces of glass to one side with her foot. She must ask Cobham to sweep the yard. Yes! She stared up at the window. That was what had been troubling her.

If the first attack had been made from the outside, why was the bulk of the glass out here and not within the room? She closed her eyes, imagining how it would be if you hit at a pane of glass and knew she was right.

'Miss Cleveland? Is something wrong?'

But how could she refuse him? Perhaps he was forming an attachment for this Sophie and her presence might distract him from any underhand activity. She was forgetting that to stay ahead of him, she must give no hint of her suspicions.

'I will consult my aunt. You understand, I do nothing without her approval. It would be unfair when she is at a time of life when she needs rest and, er, solitude.' Hoping Lady Hartness would forgive this blatant misrepresentation. At least, the excuse would give her time to think.

Lady Hartness however welcomed the news. 'Northcott? Oh, I remember the family well. Very respectable. I believe I met the children with their mother when Hartness was alive. I am never too taken with children but they were adorable. And I would not be surprised if Sophie has not turned out a beauty. I am quite excited. We have rusticated here for too long.

'But we are not prepared for entertaining. They will have to take us as they find us.'

'Oh, they will not object to anything, I'm sure. And we may easily move both Martin and Brook into the east wing and cover the damp with a picture or two and some hangings. They won't mind it.'

'Certainly I will have no compunction in moving Lord Brook. It may work, I suppose.'

'And only think of the advantages.' Her aunt's eyes were sparkling. 'If we cannot tempt you with Lord Brook, perhaps Mr Northcott will serve our purpose. Yet another gentleman with an interest in Egyptology. Who would have thought we might find so many and merely by staying at home?'

'Aunt! I cannot allow this.'

'Why not? One of them surely will prove the answer to our dilemma. Do not be too swift to decide upon Mr Martin without giving the others a fair chance. Now, leave the domestic arrangements to me and you go off and see to your collection. I know you hate to be away from it.'

Thus thrusting her into the presence of two possible suitors and making sure the collection was ready to interest the third, Nerissa thought. Finding a husband was important, of course, but she wished her aunt would leave it to her. Only a few short days ago, everything had seemed so simple.

She paused. If nothing else, maybe Sophie Northcott would come out of this with a husband? If she and Lord Brook were so well acquainted, Nerissa was surprised he had not offered for her already. But maybe his grandfather had been the obstacle. Now Lord Brook had come into his inheritance, there would be nothing to stop him. Even less now he had no longer to worry about his obligation to his dying friend, feeling that he must offer for Nerissa. I have done him a favour, Nerissa thought. Now he is free to marry who he wants.

And so was she. Poor brave Mr Martin, suffering danger and injury in her service. He had proved himself suitable in every way. Why trouble about Lord Brook when she had Martin to protect her? Together they must be more than a match for him.

She set off to present the servants with another task, feeling that she hardly liked to ask it of the conscientious Wilkins. 'But do please tell them to concentrate on the most important rooms, keeping the work to a minimum. They do not need to dust the books in the library for example. I have noticed that someone has been tidying and re-arranging in there and while I commend their efforts, they have more than enough to do already.'

Martin did not linger in his room any longer than a few hours of lost sleep required. He was down in the steward's room before luncheon, his head bandaged and his face pale but determined. Nerissa was pleased that her heart beat faster at the sight of him as she felt the warmth rushing to her cheeks. Yes, she was right. He must be the one.

She stood up, reaching out her hands. 'There was no need to come down so soon. I have checked and re-organised everything. Nothing is missing and very little damaged. They tried and failed to get into the other crates but they were packed too well — perhaps that was the noise Lord Brook heard.' If she were able to believe his version of events. 'It was all worse than it looked.'

'Where is he now?'

'He has taken notice at last and ridden over to Wellsthorpe where I hope he will find much to occupy him. So, I am afraid there is little for you to do here.'

'But surely, we must press on? The work is now even more urgent. We must open up those crates and see for ourselves what is tempting these villainous attacks. Once that is done, you will be safe.'

'I suppose so.' Nerissa regarded the crates. 'I had not thought of that.'

Martin groaned. She stepped over to him, her hand hovering over his forehead. 'I knew it. Your wound is painful.'

'No, not at all. I'm suffering the pain

of knowing myself responsible. You entrusted me with guarding the collection and I let you down.'

'Nonsense.' Nerissa reached up to rearrange the edges of the bandage. 'The blood is contained. I think it has stopped bleeding. We will leave it for the moment and I will dress it again later today.'

'I want to be rid of it. It is a badge of my inadequacy.'

'Your forehead is warmer than I would like. Do you feel feverish?'

'Only because I am standing so close to you,' Martin murmured.

'Yes,' Nerissa whispered. 'I also.' Instinctively, she raised her face as he lowered his. It was inevitable that their lips must meet. She closed her eyes, holding her breath.

'There you are, Martin,' Lord Brook cried, bounding in. 'I looked for you earlier.'

They broke apart. Nerissa was flushing with anger. She stumbled backwards on to one of the crates and both men reached out to steady her but to her annoyance, Lord Brook's arm grasped her first. 'I did not look to see you here this morning.' She spoke with as much dignity as she could manage.

'Evidently,' Lord Brook said, straight-faced. 'But believe me, I shall never be far away while I sense you have need of me.' He stared at her intently, as if wishing to communicate some deeper meaning. Nerissa felt herself drawn to the depths of his brown eyes. River water in flood. Deep, dark and clear. Like the pool at the foot of the Leap.

'No need at all.' Martin's voice came from far away. 'Miss Cleveland and I have perfected a system of working.'

'Indeed we have.' Nerissa shook herself out of her trance. This would not do. How were they to be rid of Lord Brook when he was so obviously insistent on remaining here? But if he were always to be present, or interrupting, how was her courtship to progress? It had hardly begun.

Nerissa sighed. She could only hope

that when the beautiful Miss Northcotts arrived, she would provide a distraction for Lord Brook. Not difficult for herself as hostess to ensure that they were together as often as possible. Lord Brook had spoken of her so warmly after all. Yes, the arrival of the Northcott would be to the benefit of everyone.

Yet strangely the prospect gave her no pleasure.

6

Nerissa was expecting to dislike at least one, if not both, her unexpected visitors but to her surprise, resenting Sophie Northcott proved impossible. She was of such a cheerful and yet thoughtful disposition that Nerissa was amazed that she and Lord Brook were not attached already.

'Oh, Miss Cleveland,' Sophie cried. 'It is so good of you to take us in at such short notice. We should have turned back straightaway, as soon as we heard of the difficulty at Wellsthorpe, but we were both concerned about Brook after his long illness and so we pressed on.'

'We wanted to see for ourselves that he had returned to health,' her brother added, cheerfully. 'He had assured us he had, in his letter, but anything may be said in a letter. You can't count on

Brook telling you the truth about something like that. Bound to be making light of it.'

'In the absence of any more satisfactory relatives, you see, we have always considered ourselves as Brook's family. Oh, I'm sorry, Brook, I am rattling on and not allowing you a word in edgeways.'

'When was that any different?' Lord Brook said with a smile. Nerissa perceived the fondness in his voice. No, she must be happy for them and allow them as much time alone as was possible. And this would be to her own advantage, with Martin.

Except that as hostess, she could hardly neglect Mr Northcott. Or strictly speaking was Lord Brook his host and responsible for his entertainment? Perhaps he would sit with Lady Hartness when required. She could be most entertaining when she chose and would want to hear about all the many and various branches of the Northcott family.

But then, Northcott was bound to be interested in the collection, she was forgetting his connection with the British Museum. Another opportunity lost, for both herself and Sophie to further their romances. She was conscious that she did not have too much time; when the crates were unpacked, Martin would have no further wish to stay. Somehow she must bring him to a declaration before too long. And if Lord Brook could be pushed into doing the same with Sophie, everyone would be happy.

But this was a kindness the lively Sophie did not seem disposed to take advantage of. Indeed, she seemed to wish the four of them to enjoy activities together. 'Sunshine at last,' she declared one morning. 'After so much rain. Perhaps we could have a walk in the grounds? I should love to explore. Brook was always full of Askley's grounds and the fun to be had.'

'The paths will still be muddy,' Nerissa said doubtfully. Mud didn't worry her but Sophie's clothes were such works of art that she would hate to see them spoiled. 'I wondered if your brother might wish to view the collection? Of course, there is still a great deal to do — Mr Northcott?'

Mr Northcott, who had been contemplating the view of the shrubbery, seemed startled. 'The collection? Oh, as always, I bow to my sister's wishes.' He turned his head and Nerissa thought he and Brook exchanged a glance. 'Eager as I am to view it, naturally. But I am sure there will be plenty of time for that. Although I am surprised you wish me to join your walk, Sophie, you always berate me for lagging behind and losing myself. I am something of a poet you see, Miss Cleveland and apt to be absent minded.'

What was she to make of that, Nerissa wondered? A hint to Brook and his sister that there would be plenty of opportunities for a tete-a-tete during a walk? Well, it might work to Nerissa's advantage too.

When Sophie had plans, they were executed swiftly it seemed. In no time, they were setting off, mud or no mud. and Mr Martin too, in spite of his diffident protests.

'Brook has told us about the family feud when the stream changed course. So tragic when the two families had been so close. May we see the stream and the waterfall, Nerissa?'

'We will be there shortly. At present we are crossing the dried-up bed where the stream originally ran. It would change course frequently when the beck was in flood. The small hill in between was considered as belonging to both — or neither — for many years.' She cast Lord Brook a rueful glance. 'But then my grandfather decided to develop the caves and form the Grotto and a convenient rock slide diverted the steam permanently.

'Old Lord Brook believed that my grandfather had engineered the slide, to Askley's advantage of course,' she added. 'He would have been perfectly capable of that, I'm afraid.'

'Oh, Brook — the Grotto could have been yours,' Sophie cried. 'Do you feel the loss deeply?'

Lord Brook laughed. 'Of course not. I never cared one way or the other. I resented my grandfather's ridiculous anger over a small portion of land.'

'How disappointing of you, Brook. Never mind, there is always the Leap.' She pulled what she obviously believed was a tragic face. 'I simply must see the Leap. It is such a romantic story. Did someone really drown there on his way to meet with his clandestine love?'

'I am afraid so,' Nerissa said. 'That's how the story goes, but there is no historical proof of it. It was during the Wars Of The Roses, our family were for the white rose of York and Brook's for Lancaster. And of course the son of the white rose fell in love with the daughter of the red. If he took the Leap boldly, they could meet here in the woods secretly. But one day, the rocks were slippery, he and his horse misjudged the distance and were both killed.'

'How desperately sad,' Sophie sighed. 'And being so, must be included in our walk so that we may suitably distress ourselves.'

Nerissa laughingly agreed. 'Of course. That has always been one of my favourite walks.'

'I really do feel that I shall make the party too unwieldy. For the paths,' Martin murmured.

'But we would not dream of setting off without you. Is there not a Grotto of Egyptian interest? We would value your company extremely in showing it to us.'

Nerissa explained about the key.

'Even better,' Sophie cried. 'A mystery. We may exclaim and express regret to our heart's content. Come, Mr Martin, admit — you will enjoy seeing where it is.'

He bowed. 'Anything that interests you.'

'Gallantly said.'

Within moments, it seemed, Sophie had organised her little party. But although she began by taking Martin's arm, as the path twisted through the copse to reveal the fine view of the gorge where the beck tumbled away from the waterfall, the positions were altered. Sophie was with Lord Brook, Nerissa with Martin — and Northcott had wandered away to exclaim at the grandeur of the view.

Sophie sighed. 'No wonder you came to blows over the ownership of all this. I should of all things love to possess a gorge and a waterfall. How I envy you, Nerissa.'

Nerissa was forced to stand close to Martin's side where the path was rocky and uneven. 'And this is the Leap.'

'Goodness, could one attempt it? Surely it is too wide, even on horseback.'

The gentlemen all assured her that it would probably be possible. Given enough speed on the approach and a reasonable mount. In another moment, Nerissa thought, they would be foolishly agreeing to prove it. She said quickly, 'This was my parents' favourite walk too. So they decided to improve upon my grandfather's original design and formed the Grotto together.'

'I can imagine it.'

'They were a very loving couple,' Nerissa murmured, almost to herself.

She led the way until the gorge became impassable, the water lost to view beyond the rocks below. They turned off along a damp path edged with ferns. A small clearing opened and beneath a natural overhang surrounded by moss and dripping water stood a stout door.

'Oh, how exquisite. And you have no idea where the key might be?'

'My father had it in his possession. I thought that either of these gentlemen might have brought it back. But in truth that was probably too simple.' She laughed. 'There will be a puzzle to solve before I find it.'

'Yet another mystery. How wonderful.' Sophie's face was alight with enthusiasm.

'I have cudgelled my brains in vain,' Nerissa admitted. 'No doubt I shall discover the answer when I am thinking of something else.'

'We could instigate a search. Do you think it might be hidden somewhere here? Under a rock? Within a hollow tree? Are there any hollow trees? If not, there should be. Perhaps your grandfather had one made, to blend cunningly with the real trees.'

'Far too simple, I assure you. No, we will be made to work harder than that.' Nerissa spoke lightly but was in fact glad that the puzzle would never be so easily solved. The Grotto was too personal, too bound up with memories of both her parents to be the climax of some fantastical game of hide and seek.

'Your grandfather used to set puzzles for us to solve when we were children,' Lord Brook said. It was as if he was a boy again as he laughed. 'But we could never outwit him, however hard we tried.'

If only, Nerissa thought. If only what?

If they were both children again without the bitterness and tragedy that had since divided them? No, now she was being selfish.

'So the answer could be anywhere — in the grounds, the outbuildings. Inside the house even — there, I have it. The perfect entertainment for inclement weather. How exciting.' Sophie's blue eyes danced. 'Have you ever been inside the Grotto? Do you know what it contains?'

'Never since my mother died. But before then, yes, I saw what was being done. It was far from finished of course. There is a huge and heavy sarcophagus that takes up a great deal of the floor space. That was what inspired their choice of the Grotto from the first, for keeping my father's discoveries. He wanted the sarcophagus in the house but my mother was adamant.' Nerissa laughed, remembering those happy times.

'A sarcophagus? Does it contain a body? The remains of a Pharaoh?'

'I am afraid it does not even have a lid. My mother suggested that it would make a more suitable container for shrubs. And there are a few statues also from my father's earlier travels. Nothing of any great interest.' She paused, for in truth she did not know what else the Grotto contained.

They began to make their way back and Nerissa took her place beside Martin. She must say something. The opportunities were all too few. 'Will you be returning to Egypt when the collection is finally handed over?'

'I expect so. Yes.' Martin seemed wary, not meeting her eyes.

'I intended joining my father out there. How I wish . . . ' Nerissa paused. The path was narrow here and they had to walk closely together. As the path twisted through the undergrowth, there were times when they were almost completely alone. She knew every turn. This was the best place.

She stopped and Martin stopped also. She raised her face to his.

Somehow an unwelcome memory intruded, of the drowning sensation she had felt on looking into Lord Brook's eyes. No, don't think of that.

He said, in a low voice. 'My future is so uncertain.'

'It need not be. If I had someone to escort me . . . '

His lips met hers. There was hunger there and passion, she was sure of it. This was what they both wanted. And yet there was something missing. Nonsense, Nerissa thought, I am being missish — and at my age.

From the corner of her eye, she saw a movement along the path behind them. Sophie and Lord Brook. As yet, they had not been seen. Sophie was gazing into her escort's face with a serious expression.

Martin had seen them too. They stepped apart, widening the gap between them as much as the surrounding bushes would allow. But it was done, Nerissa thought. Her intentions were now clear. From now on, he would be seeking for them to be alone together as much as she was and that would make things easier.

She wanted to say, 'We could go to Egypt together.' But he must speak. She had made it clear enough. And now there was no mistaking Lord Brook's frown. Had he seen them? Nerissa tossed her head. Why should she care what he thought? She was in love and that was all that mattered. Her heart was beating rapidly and her cheeks were flushed with elation. A sure sign of love. There could be no doubt.

Sophie however was now her usual self and without Nerissa knowing how it had happened, the two women were walking arm in arm, leaving Martin to Lord Brook. At least Mr Northcott had now appeared also, so hopefully Lord Brook would not begin haranguing poor Martin again.

'I am so conscious that we have visited ourselves upon you and are disrupting your lives,' Sophie said. 'Worthy though our motives are.'

Nerissa managed a laugh. 'Perhaps I needed a little gentle disruption. I have become very set in my ways.'

'Never. You do yourself an injustice. You sound as if you are describing a spinster aunt and you are very far from that fate, I can assure you.'

'Certainly, because I have no brothers or sisters.' But she was none too happy that the possibility had even occurred to Sophie. Was that the impression she gave, closeted here with her work? 'But I take your meaning. And I do have further plans. I mean to travel in my father's footsteps and go to Egypt.'

The prospect had never seemed so close. And yet had she given too much away? What if Sophie proffered her assistance in bringing Martin to a proposal? She was a young lady difficult to argue with once her mind was made up, much as Nerissa liked her.

Sophie merely gave her a meaningful look. 'Ah, do not worry, we shall not interfere with your duties. My brother and I are very easily pleased. We can walk and sketch and read. And work at solving Askley's mysteries.'

Nerissa sighed her relief. Perhaps Sophie was more sensitive than she had suspected. Warmly, she tried to offer more. 'Maybe we could have a musical evening?'

'With dancing? Oh, yes. We could make three couples — if Lady Hartness would dance? Northcott would make her a charming partner.'

Nerissa had intended something more sedate, around the piano. 'Oh, yes, indeed. But Lord Brook? Does he dance?' Nerissa could not hide her surprise.

Sophie laughed. 'I am sure he would tell you otherwise but he enjoyed excellent tuition when staying with us. I will not allow him to pretend he has forgotten.'

Suddenly Nerissa could not welcome the intimacy of three couples and watching Lord Brook exercising his dancing skills with Sophie — and she had no idea of Mr Martin's accomplishments. A happy thought occurred to her. 'But it is the time of year for the assemblies to begin at the Royal Oak in Bailford. Would that not be better?'

'The very thing! When is the next one?' On hearing that it would take place, when Nerissa had thought for a few moments, within the following week, Sophie was ecstatic. 'Of course we must go. It will knock Brook out of his sullens and prove a tonic for all of us.'

And the perfect opportunity for Martin to make a declaration, Nerissa thought. The intimacy that could be achieved within a crowd would be ideal for her purpose.

'Thank you so much,' Sophie was saying. 'I never thought that our stay here would be so enjoyable.' Her face was alive with delight.

Ideal also for Lord Brook to declare himself? Well, after years of obvious devotion it was what Sophie deserved. And Nerissa must wish them well.

7

Although the forthcoming outing to the Assembly was proving a welcome distraction, Nerissa knew that she could no longer put off the moment she dreaded. It was surely only due to his excellent manners that Mr Northcott had not asked. She must invite him to view the collection.

The group arranged themselves in the room, made even smaller when Wilkins had brought chairs for the ladies — for Sophie and even Lady Hartness would not be left out. Nerissa had a feeling of dread. She felt as if she would be baring her soul; she could not welcome the experience. They would be bored, disappointed — Northcott might view the objects as nothing out of the ordinary. Supposing the museum did not want them?

A foolish thought. Nerissa knew that

as soon as she had begun. Her audience were rapt, attending to every word. From time to time, Brook or Martin would make a valid comment. At times they seemed so much in accord as they discussed the tombs at Asyut or the difficulties of translating the newly-discovered Rosetta Stone that one would never have guessed an ill feeling between them.

'The Rosetta Stone?' Sophie asked. 'I think I have heard of it. What is it?'

'A stone which holds the same transcript repeated three times in different languages,' Lord Brook explained. 'Because we are able to read some of them, it holds the clue to understanding Egyptian hieroglyphs.'

'It was discovered by Napoleon's party of scholars,' Martin said. 'But the English now have it.'

'My father had done a considerable amount of work on the translation before he died,' Nerissa said.

'So the opportunity is there for someone to continue and make the all-important discovery.' Sophie clasped her hands together.

'Indeed, but the notes are lost,' Lord Brook said shortly. He gave Nerissa a sidelong glance.

She gasped in annoyance. Surely he did not feel she was keeping them from him purposely? But then, if she had known where they were, was that not exactly what she would have done? She smiled, her ill humour dispelled. 'No doubt they will turn up. I feel that they are here somewhere. I doubt whether he would have entrusted the notes to the crates.'

'No, indeed,' Martin said swiftly. 'I think that most unlikely, the perils of the journey, too great a risk.'

'Unfortunately,' Lord Brooks said, 'part of the Rosetta Stone is also missing. When it was found, embedded in an old wall, it was incomplete. This is why interpreting the writing on it has proved more difficult than expected.' He gave another of his unreadable looks, encompassing both Nerissa and

Martin. 'I have heard it said that if the missing piece could be recovered, it would be worth its weight in diamonds.'

'I am sure it would be,' Nerissa said crisply, 'but as we do not have it, that is mere speculation.' Why must he persist in these cryptic comments? Surely he did not think that she had it and was concealing it from him?

Sophie was holding a particularly fine depiction of a hunting scene on papyrus. 'If only we could know,' she said wistfully. 'What secrets might be revealed?'

'Indeed,' her brother said cordially. 'We would know who these people were, what they were doing, what they are holding . . . '

Nerissa glanced at him in surprise. Was his experience of Egyptian objects less than she had been led to believe? Surely someone with his experience of the museum must recognise the subject?

'Do you consider it to compare favourably with other examples of hunting scenes, Northcott?' Lord Brook said quickly. 'The details and colouring are very fine.'

Northcott cleared his throat and seemed to recollect himself. 'Oh, comparable, certainly. I would hope that this piece might be displayed in London. Indeed, as much of the collection as might be spared. I am most impressed.'

The conversation became more general and Northcott was able to express a lively opinion on whether the English or French might be first to decipher the Rosetta Stone.

'For although we hold the stone now,' Nerissa explained to Sophie, 'the French would have taken plaster casts of it before losing both the stone and the Battle Of The Nile to the British.'

'Ah, brave Lord Nelson,' Lady Hartness murmured.

'Yes, we must never underestimate Bonaparte and his resources,' Northcott said. 'What do you say, Martin?'

Mr Martin shrugged. 'We were

fortunate enough to avoid the French when we were camped near Alexandria.'

'But you must have an opinion.'

Martin shook his head. 'It is in the hands of fate. To me, gaining the knowledge is what is important — and that the information should be shared. Not who gains the glory of making the discovery.'

'Bravo,' Nerissa said warmly. 'My father's sentiments exactly.' She smiled her encouragement. 'Lord Brook, if you were to choose one item out of everything unpacked so far, what would it be?' She merely wished to direct the conversation away from Martin but Lord Brook entered into the game with enthusiasm.

'An almost impossible task amongst so many fascinating objects.'

Nerissa was already trying to keep from looking at her own favourite, lest she gave the game away. But it was as if he had read her thoughts. Lord Brook's fingers went at once to a serpentine drinking vessel, holding it delicately. 'This is lovely. I have always thought so.'

'My favourite too,' Nerissa said softly. As she took the sinuously graceful cup from him, his fingers brushed her hand. Startled, she looked up and their eyes met. He was smiling down at her and the tenderness in his eyes was no longer directed at the item of his choice.

'I would choose this,' Martin said, reaching for a funeral figure. Nerissa hardly saw what he took; the moment was broken. Her mind was a turmoil of emotion. What had happened? Her heart was beating so fast that she was certain Lord Brook must notice. Indeed, all of them must.

She made herself look away from him, keeping the conversation light and general, befitting her role as hostess, hardly hearing what anyone said. 'My father had an extensive collection of books about Egypt — almost everything that has ever been published on the subject. Any of you are welcome to use the library whenever you wish. Although they are not in any very logical order I am afraid. I cannot seem to find some of them, my father's favourite copy of Herodotus, for example.'

'Indeed, we are all familiar with Herodotus,' Lord Brook said easily. 'The father of history. Much of our information about the Egyptians has been gained from him, has it not, Northcott?'

Mr Northcott bowed his assent.

'Father of history and father of lies,' Mr Martin said. 'Unfortunately his version of events is not to be relied upon.'

'Which is why we need to translate the hieroglyphs,' Lord Brook said. 'And why Giles Cleveland's work is so vital.'

Nerissa was hardly listening. She thought, in a moment of amazed wonder, I love him. I know it. But I can't, I have planned to marry Mr Martin, have been working towards that goal for days, weeks, but I have loved Brook almost from the first moment of meeting him again, from the seeds sown in childhood friendship. For all his faults. Besides, she knew now that she had misjudged him. The shyness she had often mistaken for arrogance masked integrity and kindness.

And perhaps — might the look in his eyes mean that her feelings were returned, at least a little? Slowly she became calmer and recognised the truth as Brook turned to answer a laughing query from Sophie. No, he could never be hers. She was too late. His heart belonged to Sophie and rightly so. Sophie who could cheer him out of the sullens with a single word or a smile.

Nerissa knew now the meaning of the niggling feelings she had experienced on observing the two together. Nothing less than jealousy. And all her own fault.

One might say how fortunate that having turned down Lord Brook's proposal, she had another suitor in the wings. No, she thought at once. Having recognised her love for one man, she would not settle for less with anyone else.

It would not be fair, either for Martin or herself. Perhaps she might return to her original idea and suggest that Martin might accompany herself and Lady Hartness of Egypt as escort? She would immerse herself in the fascination of the work there and forget what might have been.

It would have been easy to resent Sophie if she had not been such a loveable girl, always happy, always unstinting in her praise and thought for others. Only once did the joyful features slip and then only for a moment.

As Nerissa came down into the hall one morning, Sophie was asking Wilkins if the post had been fetched that day? And upon hearing that it had, she turned away from the butler's shaking head almost with a look of despair. But as she saw Nerissa, she resumed the joyful smile.

'I have been meaning to ask you, because we do not have much time.

What will you wear to the assembly? Because we must make sure to compliment each other. As I am fashionably fair but unfashionably plump, I always need to consider my companions with care, I do assure you. But your dark curls and slim figure will set me off quite well, I believe.' This was said with such a ridiculous look that Nerissa had to laugh.

'I have a problem,' Nerissa said. 'I have consulted with my aunt and we have decided that since it is several months since my father's actual death, half-mourning will be permissible on this occasion. But I do not possess anything very fashionable, as it is some time now since Lady Hartness escorted me through my seasons. That ended when Lord Hartness died and their London house had to be given up.'

Before she had even finished speaking, Sophie had seized her hand and was leading her upstairs. 'I am sure I will have the very thing . . . see. How about this? White with silver thread embroidery is always acceptable and the train is not too full. And being a little large for you, my maid will easily take it in.'

'I thought I would wear the pendant my father gave me,' Nerissa said. She would feel that he was near her. 'It is lapis lazuli and therefore dark blue-green in colour.'

'So the white will show it off admirably. And listen, now I insist you must humour me in this, before we set off, we shall enter the drawing room together. We shall be the perfect foil for one another.'

Sophie was right. A few evenings later as they entered the room, Nerissa knew that she looked well. Under Sophie's skilful hands, her dark curls were clustered over a blue ribbon, exactly matching the hue of the heavy pendant and accentuating the blue of Nerissa's eyes.

'There!' Sophie cried. 'You are all to admire my handiwork.'

Three heads turned. Northcott's

smile was uncomplicated and appreciative. As was Martin's, indeed, she had never seen such a look of enthusiasm on the handsome face. But her attention was concentrated on Lord Brook, who nodded with his usual solemn stare before he too smiled. Nerissa's heart leapt.

'Undoubtedly,' Northcott said gallantly. 'But you were working from good material if I may say so. You were merely gilding the lily. What do you say, Brook?'

Lord Brook mumbled something. And of course, Nerissa realised with a sickening lurch, she was standing next to Sophie. It was Sophie, in her delicate sapphire silk who had inspired his first reaction. It had been foolishness on Nerissa's part to expect anything else.

Impossible however, not to be caught up in Sophie's enthusiasm for the evening. There were already several other parties approaching the Royal Oak as they arrived. The landlord's delight was evident; if anyone had thought the first assembly of the season was being held a little early, he was already justified.

Again, the brother and sister seemed determined to organise them all. 'Come, Martin, do not be hanging back,' Mr Northcott said in a kindly tone. 'Put your name on Miss Cleveland's card. There, see.'

'Yes, I did not mean to be hesitant. It is the lights, I am sometimes afflicted at occasions such as these.' He did indeed look pale.

Nerissa was immediately remorseful. 'Oh, you should have told us. But of course, we gave you no chance to object.'

'No matter. I shall come about,' Mr Martin said bravely.

'Why trouble to mention it then?' Lord Brook muttered and earned a tap on the hand from Sophie's fan.

'What a stir we are causing,' Lady Hartness said with a wicked chuckle as she took a seat by the fire. 'No-one expected us or knows who our companions are, and they must all come to be enlightened. Lady Barrington's nose will be quite out of joint. She cannot bear to be behind with the gossip.'

Nerissa laughed as Northcott led her away for the first set. It was good to see her aunt enjoying herself so much. I have been remiss, she thought, in not considering her feelings when I chose to avoid socialising. But her laughter died at the sight of Sophie as the partner of Lord Brook. She said lightly, 'They make a handsome couple, do they not?'

Northcott glanced over his shoulder as the steps brought them together. 'No doubt . . . if they could argue less. My sister teases Brook unmercifully, always has done. But it does him good. He's far too solemn.'

Nerissa need only nod as the dance bore her away for Lord Brook was now smiling at Sophie. Ridiculous that this should affect her so much when only days ago, Nerissa had thought she could not abide the man.

The two dances ended and the two

couples arrived back at Lady Hartness's side at the same time. Sophie's fan was in action again. 'Now, Brook, as I instructed. No backing away.'

Lord Brook was no longer smiling. 'Miss Cleveland, I must speak with you. If we might sit the next dance out . . . '

Nerissa's fingers trembled as she looked at her card. 'Mr Martin is next. And he has not yet danced.'

Of course, Brook must have declared himself to Sophie. Nerissa would be expected to free him once and for all from her father's foolish obligation and wish them joy. It was impossible. She said, 'Afterwards, maybe, when it is your turn.'

Lord Brook bent his head towards hers. 'I must speak. Miss Northcott tells me I am blunt and a clumsy fool and she is right. I can only pray I have not irreparably ruined my suit.'

Suit? Nerissa thought. What could he mean? She lifted her eyes to his to see a look of yearning there. She could not be mistaking the depth of his feeling. Could she?

But Martin was at her elbow. 'Miss Cleveland? My dance, I believe?' His voice was hesitant, but she could not disappoint him.

Lord Brook muttered something. His fingers brushed hers and she and Martin swung away for the set was forming and they must take their places.

'Are you quite well?' Martin sounded concerned. She realised she had missed her step for the second time and murmured something about the heat. A mistake as he was at once all sympathy and leading her away from the floor, leaving the set to its own devices.

He understood only too well, she must not dance while feeling faint. The grip on her arm was surprisingly strong as he led her into a small parlour, set for cards but at present empty and pleasantly cool. 'Might I fetch you some lemonade?'

'No, thank you. I am completely

recovered now. I think we may return to the ballroom after all.'

To her surprise he seized her hand in both of his. 'I must speak. When I felt you stumble in the dance and saved you from falling, I knew beyond doubt.' He placed an arm around her shoulders.

'Mr Martin, please.'

'I can contain my feelings no longer. Miss Cleveland, I beg you to be my wife.' His lips were upon hers, pressing her back against his arms, as if he was assuming her answer must be yes. But how could it be? Not now, when she loved Lord Brook. Her pendant was pulling against her throat; it must have caught in his sleeve.

This angered her most of all. She gave a muffled cry and pushed at his shoulders, twisting her head away. The small figures on the pendant snapped apart. 'No,' Nerissa cried and was free. She scrabbled wildly for her father's gift.

'Here,' Martin said, scooping it from the sofa. 'Allow me to have it repaired for you. I can do no less. I am sorry. I must have mistaken your feelings.'

Nerissa hardly heard his apology. Panic was rising in her throat. 'There is a piece missing. Where is it?'

'I have it,' Martin said quietly. 'I insist. I will have the necklace repaired and returned, as good as new.'

'No . . . thank you.' Her gaze locked with his. She took a deep breath to control the tears that threatened. 'There is no need. It is not broken, it is meant to come apart, though I have never fathomed the puzzle entirely.' She held out her hand for the piece he still held, aware that she was trying to say too many things at once.

He glanced at it, before shrugging and passing it to her. 'And your answer?'

'Answer?' For a moment, she could not remember what he meant. 'Oh, I am sorry. But no, I cannot marry you.'

He frowned. 'I do not understand. You have given me every indication that we should deal well together. At every opportunity, you have cited our shared interests, the pleasures of companionship. I believed you were encouraging me.'

Nerissa hesitated. 'I know. I feel I have treated you badly. I am sorry if I have misled you, but I have also been misleading myself. I do not do this lightly, believe me. There was a time when yes . . .' She stopped, feeling that she might only be making matters worse.

There was a strange look in Martin's eyes. 'I see how it is. You are promised to someone else.'

Beyond the room, she could hear the music drawing to a close. She said desperately, 'For this next dance, yes. I must go.'

'That is not what I meant and you know it.' He seized her wrist. 'I only wish to know that my rival will not be that man. That despicable ogre who cannot speak a civil word to me.'

Nerissa pulled her arm away. 'You don't understand. He is not like that at all.'

'Is this what your father would have wanted? For his close friend to be treated so shabbily?'

'Mr Martin, I am forever in your debt where my father was concerned. But I must decide for myself how best to fulfil his wishes. I must go.' She pushed him aside and hurried from the room and this time he did not try to stop her. And it was all right. The couples were still leaving the floor.

Lord Brook was looking about him, frowning but as she approached, his face lightened. 'I must repeat, I have to speak with you,' he said in a low voice.

Nerissa nodded, hardly daring to breathe and fortunately he led her to the refreshment room, almost deserted so early in the evening, and not to the small card room. She thought of Martin, still there she assumed, and how dark his thoughts might be. But surely she had never given him any real cause for hope?

Apart from that one kiss. She had been very wrong in that respect.

Otherwise, she had behaved with propriety even if her underlying motives had been far from proper.

They walked past the table with its array of light refreshments and along to one of the panelled window bays where there was a sense of seclusion. He turned to face her.

'Miss Cleveland, Nerissa, I was abrupt before, ridiculously so, but my feelings remain the same. They always will.'

His face carried that same intent look which had first touched her heart. 'I am convinced we should be well suited. I was at fault before in giving my only reason as my obligation to your father. How could I expect you to respond favourably?'

Nerissa's fingers were tight with tension. What was he saying? And what about Sophie? Was he again suggesting a convenient marriage for people who were well suited? How cold that sounded. And all the while her heart was aching with love for him. But he only regarded her as suitable — so suitable that he was willing to sacrifice his feelings for Sophie.

Lord Brook sighed. 'It is of no use,' he said gloomily. 'I can see that in your face. But please try and see this from my point of view. I arrived here dreading the task of announcing your father's death only to find nothing as I expected. I was taken aback by Martin's presence and responded badly. And you would not heed my warnings.'

'I was wrong.'

'I should have tackled my task more convincingly I think if I had not cared about you so much.'

Nerissa stared at him, thoroughly lost. 'You care about me?'

'Of course.' His look was of surprised frustration. 'Always. Since we were first intended for each other as children. When the families quarrelled I was devastated. I resolved, that in spite of the rift, I would seek you out and reclaim you as my own as soon as I came of age and could act for myself.

Perhaps at the time it was partly hurt pride that drove me.

'I was angry that our feelings should be disregarded and wished to spite my grandfather. But when I reached twenty-one, I knew that I could not come to you without a means of supporting you — and the means to help you with Askley. I realised however that I could serve you by serving your father — and that I did. And came to value him as a friend. I did not wish him to make my feelings known to you too soon, in case any hint reached my grandfather. If that had happened, all would have been lost.

'As if I cared for your inheritance.'

'I have made too many assumptions. I feel I must be completely honest with you. At first I sought out Giles Cleveland mainly to go against my grandfather's wishes but as I came to know him, my sincere respect for your father grew into friendship.'

At any other time, these sentiments would have pleased Nerissa, but not now. She was shaking her head, almost weeping. 'These are all matters of sense and reason. What about feeling? And what about Sophie? Please forget your obligation to my father; I release you entirely. You must follow your heart.' The words almost choked her and yet she could not allow him to sacrifice himself in this way.

He stared at her. 'I am trying to put things right. I am following my heart. Oh, Nerissa, can you not see it? Since returning to Askley and meeting you again, there is no doubt in my mind. Or my heart. I love you and always will. Please tell me there is hope for me. And that I have not alienated you altogether with my abruptness or manner. Or my unfortunate failure to express myself.' He moved closer, placing his hands on her arms. She could feel his breath in her hair.

Nerissa's heart was singing. 'I wouldn't want you to be any different. I love you too.'

He kissed her as she was still trying

to explain how her feelings had altered and the explanation did not matter. Nothing mattered. They were lost, aware only of each other. She responded with a passion she did not know she possessed.

There was a cough from beyond their window bay and they broke apart. Nerissa knew that her face was alight with joy and hardly cared. She wanted the whole world to know of their happiness and wish them well.

'Excuse me,' Martin said. 'Miss Cleveland, I am not at all well.' His face was white and there was a feverish glint in his eyes. He stepped backwards into the main room, gesturing that she might follow.

How much had he witnessed? Nerissa thought guiltily that he was the one person she would have wished could discover this more gently. She had no wish to hurt him. And coming upon her so soon after she had refused him.

Nerissa turned to Lord Brook. 'I won't be a moment.'

He smiled his agreement although he could not have been happy at the interruption. They were beyond Lord Brook's hearing now. She said urgently, 'I am sorry . . . '

'I wish to leave. I do not wish to cause any fuss or spoil the evening for anyone else. I will hire a horse from the inn. Please do not tell anyone.' He gestured towards Lord Brook.

'Be assured I will not. And I agree, when Miss Northcott and my aunt are enjoying themselves so much.' How thoughtful of him. She felt even more guilty about her treatment of him. No wonder the poor man felt unwell.

He nodded and left without saying anything further. Nerissa bit her lip. Had she made a promise she would be unable to keep? If Lord Brook asked her directly, what could she say? But Lord Brook had other concerns. He was frowning now. 'I hope Martin is not going to be prattling of what he saw.' He glared at the hapless Martin's departing back.

'I am sure not. Mr Martin does not prattle.'

'No. He does not seem to do much of anything. I cannot like the man. But I would not wish any harm to come to your reputation. Although our engagement will silence the gossips.'

'Indeed, yes.' Nerissa smiled up at him. 'But I think we must return to the ballroom and be seen to be dancing before too many remark on our absence.'

'Why should they? This was my dance.'

'Our dances will surely be finished by now. You will have to hand me over to another.'

'Nonsense. A ridiculous rule. Your card if you please.' Taking it, Lord Brook scrawled, *Brook* across all the remaining spaces.

'Dear me,' Nerissa murmured, smiling. 'I hope you will not be so authoritarian when we are married.'

'Knowing you, I doubt whether you will allow me the opportunity. But in this case, I see no reason to allow some other man the pleasure I have been denied for so long. I shall speak to Lady Hartness as soon as I may and then there will be none to impede us.'

None? Nerissa remembered, with a sinking heart. Martin was not the only one she needed to feel guilty about. 'Oh, here I am feeling so happy, but what about Sophie?'

'Sophie? She will be happy for us and wish us well.'

Did he not have any idea of Sophie's feelings for him? 'I thought . . . I was certain that there was an understanding between you.'

'Between me and Sophie? Good heavens, no.' He laughed. 'Only a long standing friendship. We are like brother and sister.'

Nerissa welcomed this with relief. And Northcott had seemed to support this view she remembered. But all the same, there were moments that were not entirely explained. For the moment however, she must be content and resolved to speak to Sophie when she could.

The hours swam by, the music and the flickering candles combining to become part of the waves of joy which threatened to overwhelm her. She was conscious only of Lord Brook's presence, the caressing note in his voice when he spoke only to her, an awareness of his touch when his fingers lingered upon hers or brushed her arm. She was adrift with wonderment. Surely this evening could never, never end.

And yet it must. Mr Northcott led his sister away from the set before their dance had finished. Nerissa was jolted back into concern for her friend. Sophie's face was pale; she seemed as if she might be about to faint.

Nerissa thought, our secret is out and Brook is mistaken. This is how the news has affected her.

8

They must leave, it seemed, as soon as the carriage could be brought round. Northcott said, 'But where is Martin? We cannot leave without him.'

As they were departing anyway, there was no further need for Nerissa to remain silent. She explained what had happened but was surprised by the glances that Brook and Northcott exchanged. 'I am at fault,' Lord Brook muttered. 'Of course, when he sought you out, earlier. I hardly gave the fellow a thought, beyond wishing him anywhere else but where he was. I wanted only to be rid of him.'

'No, I too was only intent on enjoying myself,' Northcott said. 'It did not occur to me that he might leave.'

This was dreadful. She had hurt not one, but two people she cared for. Would either Martin or Sophie remain her friends after this evening? As the women collected their shawl, Nerissa murmured, 'I am so sorry. I hoped you would not, I mean, please do not feel badly of us.' She was not even certain that Sophie had heard her properly.

'No, it is nothing,' Sophie said. 'It is the heat. I am often afflicted like this. And I am sorry it should happen now and that I should spoil your evening. It is just . . . ' She seemed to wish to say more.

'We must speak at length tomorrow when you are recovered,' Nerissa said.

'Yes. I should like to tell you. When I feel stronger.'

Nerissa sighed. It must be as she had feared. But if they could have a talk and clear matters between them, it might well help. She just hoped that this would not spoil their friendship. But how could it not? She had only known Sophie for a week or two and yet she would miss her.

As they reached Askley, both Sophie and Lady Hartness declared that they would retire at once. Nerissa's offer of help was refused but with a tremulous smile. Wilkins appeared in the hallway, intent on assuring them that nothing had occurred while they had been gone. 'And Martin?' Lord Brook asked.

'Mr Martin returned some two hours ago and went straight to his room. I took him some refreshment and I believe he went straight to bed.'

'Thank you, Wilkins,' Nerissa said. 'So you see, Mr Martin arrived safely. There was no need to concern ourselves.'

'Nevertheless, I'll look in on him,' Northcott said. 'It will put our minds at rest.'

A kindness? Nerissa wondered. Or something else? But she was too weary now to worry about it.

'I forgot,' Wilkins said, 'he went first to the library. Wanting a book to help him sleep.'

'In his state of health?' Lord Brook said. Nerissa could sense his sudden alertness. 'Surely a book would be the last thing he would want?' But Northcott was already returning down the stairs. 'Sleeping like a babe,' he said cheerfully. 'Never heard me.'

Lord Brook opened the library door. 'What could he be wanting in here?' But all was as usual. The shelves revealed no secrets. He shook his head.

'What is it?' Nerissa asked. She could not be angry with him, not tonight but surely he was once again being over protective? 'Everything seems as it should be.'

'Is anything missing?'

'No.' She could see at a glance that all the shelves were filled. All? 'Ah — in fact, something that was missing has come back. My father's copy of Herodotus. I have been looking for it everywhere.'

'I cannot like this. Something is making me uneasy. But no matter.' He smiled suddenly. 'After tonight's events, all my senses are aware. You have made me the happiest man alive.' He raised her hand to his lips and held it longer than courtesy demanded. Her flesh quivered at the signal that passed between them. 'Goodnight, my love.'

Nerissa passed her aunt's door, treading carefully to avoid the creaking floorboards and knew suddenly how the volume of Herodotus had reappeared. Of course, it had been the volume now replaced by young Jack Bartlett's handsome doorstopper. She almost laughed aloud at the simplicity of her discovery. She would look forward to sharing it with the gentlemen in the morning.

Once in her room, she removed her pendant, smiling as she remembered the sensation of Brook's hands brushing her skin as he had fastened the gold and enamel clasp. She took the broken piece from her reticule, examining the fitting. Yes, it would be easy enough to repair, despite the rough treatment. She had not been aware of this; her brave words to Martin had been merely to prevent him taking it.

She turned the small, once conjoined

figures over, examining how they had fallen apart. The piece she had thought broken had been holding them together. She stared at the two pieces she now held. She had known, had she not, that there was more to this than had first appeared? She should have examined the pendant more thoroughly. This was the true puzzle. What was to happen next? She arranged and re-arranged the two pieces, her weariness forgotten.

Now that Martin had unwittingly shown her the way, the puzzle was simple. She held the pieces back to back and was rewarded as they clicked together as had always been intended. And now she was holding a key.

Tears of elation came to her eyes. She felt so close to her father in that moment. As if she had never been far from his loving guidance. She placed the pieces beneath her pillow, to be all the closer to the happy memories they held. She was almost certain that they formed the key to the Grotto. Tomorrow she and Brook together would try it.

At the last moment she moved the key and placed it on the small table beside her bed, not wishing to risk losing the pieces within the bed linen.

She had thought herself too excited to sleep but her last waking thought was of deep happiness and Lord Brook's lips upon hers.

She woke frowning into the darkness, straining her ears into the silence. The air seemed alive with small, secret currents, almost as if she could hear someone breathing.

Someone was there, in the room.

She froze into the warm sheets, every muscle tense, aching to see and hear. If only she had left her curtains open, allowing the moonlight to enter. But to reach the curtains, she would have to leave the safety of the bed.

No, this was ridiculous. Nerissa took a long slow breath and forced herself to relax. There. Nothing stirred. An over-active imagination, brought on by the evening's excitements. The room was empty.

Into the silence, her door slammed.

Nerissa sat up, biting her lips to keep back a shriek. Nothing else. Gradually, she relaxed. How foolish, to be fearful of a banging door. Many of the doors in the house slipped their catches and banged at the slightest hint of a breeze. A sudden lone guest had caused it, she told herself firmly.

She flexed and tightened her fingers to control the silly way in which they were shaking and lit a candle. Now she could see for a certain distance but the shadows at the edges of the room were even blacker than before.

Nothing else for it. She must at least shut the door properly or be woken for the rest of the night. She slid out of bed, certain that her heart was thudding more loudly than any door. She was there, safely.

She opened the door and peered out into the corridor. All was quiet. And she was not alone, she told herself. The merest cry and her own gallant protector would come to her aid in an instant. If she shouted loudly enough, even the men guarding the collection would hear. There was nothing to worry about.

She awoke to Betty opening her curtains, thinking only of her new joy and that she must hurry down to see Brook. Everything seemed so ordinary as she dressed quickly, giving hardly a thought to her night-time fears. How surprised Brook would be to hear her tale and that they had possessed the key all along. Smiling, she turned to the table where she had left it. It was not there.

Perhaps Betty had moved it, she thought wildly. Perhaps it had fallen on to the carpet. She scrabbled around the polished legs and beneath the bed for several minutes, unwilling to reach the obvious conclusion. A cold chill was brushing the back of her neck. Someone had been here.

She must find Brook and Northcott at once and tell them. Or Brook. How did she know they could trust Northcott?

He was Brook's friend but Lord Brook might have been deceived by him. Quickly she clasped the remaining part of the pendant and chain around her throat. Incongruous with a morning dress but she could not bear to let it out of her sight.

And this wretched creature who had stolen the key. Had whoever it was solved the puzzle already? If so, the Grotto lay open to them. It was even more urgent now that she must find Lord Brook. They must go there at once.

She was to be disappointed. There was only Wilkins downstairs, keeping his loyal vigil over the collection. Lord Brook's men had returned to Wellsthorpe, he told her.

There had been an urgent message about the roof and Lord Brook had followed them as soon as he came down.

'And Mr Northcott?'

'He took an early breakfast and went out, Miss. On horseback.'

Nerissa frowned. If he was making for the Grotto, why take a horse? Unless he intended to take what he could and leave straightaway. Using the opportunity of Lord Brook being occupied elsewhere.

She must go to the Grotto at once. But who else might go with her? She was reluctant to take any of the servants from their duties when they were so overstretched. It would not be fair when she was asking so much of them as it was.

She came into the hall as Mr Martin was silently leaving the library, a book under one arm. 'Good morning,' Nerissa called. 'Are you fully recovered?'

He started and the book fell to the floor. 'Yes, I am. Fully. Thank you.'

'I'm sorry,' Nerissa said. 'Your poor head. I called too loudly.' She bent for the book, which had fallen open, spine upwards. 'Why, Mr Martin, you have found the Herodotus for yourself after all. I meant to tell you . . . ' Her voice died away. The pages of the book had been cut away to form a hidden compartment. She looked up at his face, now showing concern.

'I was bringing this to show you,' Martin said. 'Something has obviously been hidden here. But now it is empty.'

'But what?' Nerissa was thinking quickly. Not the key. What else? Oh, no. She put a hand to her throat. 'The notes. My father's notes about the Rosetta Stone. What else could it be?'

'The key we have all been searching for perhaps?'

'No. I have found the key — and lost it again almost at once. Or, it has been stolen.'

'Who could have done this? Both thefts?'

'I don't know.' Nerissa was still trying to take everything in. 'I now know that I can trust Lord Brook implicitly and that leave — Mr Martin, tell me frankly, what do you think of Mr Northcott?'

'He seems pleasant enough. He has

always been polite and charming but I have to admit, in spite of his claims to be connected with the museum, he does not seem to know a great deal about Egyptian antiquities.'

Nerissa sighed. 'I have to agree. And now he has set off on horseback, while Lord Brook is distracted. I am very much afraid that the Grotto may be in danger.' Although had he not had enough, she thought bitterly with her father's notes, the work of years? He would be able to claim the glory of deciphering the Rosetta Stone for himself, with little or no effort. 'Mr Martin, will you come with me to the Grotto? I must see for myself. Perhaps I am worrying without cause but I must know.'

'Of course.' Mr Martin agreed at once. At least you could count on him for that. She smiled briefly, knowing that Lord Brook would have made all kinds of objections in his concern for her safety.

They left the house. Nerissa began to

explain how she had found the key as they walked. 'What are we to do when we get there?' Martin asked. 'Are we to conceal ourselves and wait for the intruder, hoping we may be there first?'

'If it is Northcott, I suspect that to be unlikely. I am very much afraid that all we can do is inspect the damage . . . and the loss.'

They came through the shrubbery. Nerissa exclaimed her relief. 'Nothing has been touched. Everything is the same. Or I think it is.' Perhaps after all, the ivy around the doorway had been torn.

'Perhaps we should try the door. Your villain may be inside already.'

'Oh! I see. Do you think so? How fortunate that you came with me. I should have blundered in.'

'Shall I try the door first?'

'Oh, no. I have a great deal I wish to say to this person, whoever he is. To cause all this trouble, not to mention the distress caused to me, in entering my father's most secret and private place without my permission.' They were there. Nerissa grasped the handle. 'It is still locked,' she began — and everything around her went dark.

9

Nerissa awoke with candlelight flickering above her and both her elbows scraping on rough stone. She was partly enclosed in a stone box. She tried to lift her head, was almost overwhelmed by a wave of dizziness and sank down again.

She must be inside the Grotto. And it would seem, inside the sarcophagus.

'Ah, you are awake,' a voice said. 'Good. I was beginning to think that I must take my leave while you slept. And that would be a pity because I want you to know why I have acted as I have and in whose cause.'

Nerissa managed to move a hand to her head, trying vainly to still the jarring pain. Who was this? The voice was harsh and decisive but seemed familiar. This must be the intruder. But if so, what had happened to Mr Martin?

If only she could think straight. 'Who are you?'

'I was right, you cannot even recognise my voice. You have made it plain all along how you despised me. Strange because you would have considered marriage with me when it suited you. It is Bernard Martin, Miss Cleveland.'

Nerissa closed her eyes. So this was in part her own fault. She had hurt him more deeply than she had ever realised. 'I am sorry for that. Sincerely so. My only excuse is that I did not understand my own heart. But I have never despised you.'

'No? Perhaps I know you better than you know yourself. But no matter.'

Nerissa gritted her teeth, grasped the edges of the sarcophagus and pulled herself up into a sitting position. She had to face him even though she was half fainting with the attempt. He was obviously a most dangerous man and she would have to keep her wits about her in order to escape.

Martin was seated on the stone ledge that ran along both sides of the small chamber. 'I was sorry to place you in that sarcophagus but you see, the floor space was already occupied.' He kicked out somewhere below Nerissa's field of vision and she heard a low moan. She gasped and, disregarding her own pain, peered over the edge.

Lord Brook lay crumpled between the sarcophagus and the wall, with blood on his forehead. His eyes were closed. In that moment of anguish, Nerissa regained her strength. She thought quickly. Longing to help Lord Brook, she fought against the impulse. If she feigned weakness, she would be more likely to catch Martin off-guard. As she must.

At least Brook was alive. And it was now up to her to get both of them out of this. 'What do you want?' she whispered, pressing a hand to her brow.

'What do I want?' He laughed harshly. 'Why, to see French honour restored. You English are despicable, tramping around Egypt, stealing antiquities that were rightfully ours and calling this the fortunes of war. And worst of all, to take the Rosetta stone. The honour of deciphering the code must and shall belong to the French, and when I return to serve the Emperor Napoleon Bonaparte, he will honour me as I rightfully deserve.'

Nerissa could not take everything in. 'You are working for Bonaparte? The Corsican General?' But of course, Martin was right, he had proclaimed himself Emperor now.

'You English, always refusing to recognise greatness. He will achieve more, believe me. Soon he will rule the whole of Europe.' There was a wild enthusiasm in his voice. Nerissa shivered.

Martin's shoulders twitched and it was as if he recalled where he was and who he was talking to. 'Sadly, I am not working for him officially. Not yet. But soon I shall be, when I have proved my worth.'

'So you are French,' Nerissa said dully. 'I must be very stupid. I did not know.'

'I did not wish you to know. I despised my parents — they represented the worst of the society the glorious revolution suppressed. Our family escaped to England when I was a small child. My elder brother, their favourite, died on the journey. They never forgave me for surviving. But I do not wish to speak of them. My future is with Bonaparte.'

She did not like the feverish glint that appeared in his eyes whenever he mentioned that name. She must distract him somehow. And if only she could discover the extent of Lord Brook's injuries. 'This is fascinating and I wish to hear more but I am feeling faint — there may be water in the stone basin in the corner? It gathers naturally after rainfall, I remember.' She rested her head upon the stone rim, weakly proffering her handkerchief, not daring to look at him.

He did not speak for a long moment. 'Dear me, quite the languishing female. Who would have thought it? But I do not wish you to swoon before you have heard the full account of my achievements here.' He took the scrap of fabric she offered.

As soon as he turned away, she reached downwards, placing her fingers on to Lord Brook's forehead. His flesh was still warm and she could feel a pulse beating in his temple. As she peered down at him, he opened his eyes. Nerissa almost fainted in reality, with relief. As she smiled at him, placing a warning finger to her lips, he winked. She resumed her drooping posture, hiding her smile.

Only a moment but everything was changed. Now she had hope. Anything must be possible.

Martin returned and pushed the handkerchief carelessly into her hand. 'When I first introduced myself to your father, he seemed reluctant to trust me. I despaired of ever gaining anything to help me achieve Bonaparte's favour. But when he was feverish, he began to babble about his greatest discovery — the missing portion of the Rosetta Stone. How many years of work would be saved through having those missing words? And of course the work is done almost entirely — I have your father's notes.'

Nerissa gasped. 'What are you saying? That my father discovered the missing piece somehow? But he would have told me. He would have made his discovery known.'

'Perhaps you did not know your father as well as you thought, Miss Cleveland. In my experience, every man has a flaw. And this was his. I did not know where the stone could be. I thought it must be in one of the crates Brook had despatched. I decided I would follow them here, gain your trust and discover the stone. At one point I even intended to gain everything through entirely lawful processes.'

'Lawful?' Nerissa murmured.

'Yes. Oh, I understood at once where your thoughts were leading you. And I was tempted. We could have married, returned to Egypt and been accepted by the English occupation. But I would naturally have remained in Bonaparte's service. Everything I found could have gone directly to Paris. Who knows what wealth and preferment we might have gained? And also, once married I would have avoided ever being conscripted into the French army. My talents lie elsewhere. I have no intention of suffering the fate of a common soldier.'

'Bonaparte's service?' Nerissa could not disguise her horror. 'You expected me to join with you in this?'

'Exactly, there was the flaw in my plan. You would have become a hindrance. Just as well maybe that this oaf appeared and ruined that project.' He glared down at Lord Brook. 'I had been willing to move slowly, allowing our relationship to grow, going through those crates one by one, and a weary task you made of it. But it became impossible with Brook and his friends and servants hovering around me.'

'The attacks that night? They were your doing?'

'You flatter me. One only was mine.'

'Of course, the second time, you were attacked yourself.'

'No, the second attack was my own. Easy enough to fake an injury. A moment's self-inflicted pain in a glorious cause. I had nothing to do with the first. I should ask your worthy lord about that — ah, but he is beyond speech. A pity.' He laughed. 'And all the time what I sought had been within my reach. I have the notes, concealed imperfectly in that book, and now I have the missing parts of the Rosetta Stone too. It is in several pieces and was awaiting me here all along.'

He gestured to the alcove behind her. 'Don't try to twist your head. To no avail anyway as I have everything safely in my bag. I thought at first that the pendant you wore would be a welcome addition. A gift for a very great lady

— the Empress of the greatest nation. And a gift that would bring good fortune according to Egyptian legend. But that was merely a cheap replica and therefore unworthy of the Empress Josephine.'

Nerissa's hands flew to her throat, as if gripping the gold chain for reassurance. 'But there are several things I don't understand.' If only she could delay him, keeping him boasting of his cleverness, surely Northcott would come in search of them? 'Were my father's notes concealed in that book? And how did you discover them?'

'A long and tedious search, I can assure you. At first, I had free access to the library and might take as long as I liked, undiscovered, using one of the convenient passages you told me of and which led straight there from my room. Until you decided you must move me in favour of Miss Northcott. You see, you have thwarted me at every turn.'

'I trusted you,' Nerissa said bitterly.

'Trust?' He laughed harshly. 'What is

one more subtle deceit to a family who have always applauded deception? Think of my cleverness as merely another game which you have unfortunately lost. And now, I have answered enough questions. You may work out the rest for yourself. You will have plenty of time for that. Or do you seek merely to delay me?

'Yes, I can see that you do. Your face is so expressive. But when Mr Northcott returns from his wild goose chase, he will read the note from his friend explaining how he has ridden off for a special licence, to York I believe I said. That will explain his absence. And who will be expecting you to be up so early after the excitement of the ball? Do not look to Miss Northcott, she has other concerns. Wondering why her beloved did not arrive at the assembly when she had had word that he would attend. I needed to distract her; that young lady is far too perceptive for my liking. Oh, yes, I have studied all of you and discovered your weak points and made use of them.'

Nerissa said hopelessly, 'But Northcott will know Lord Brook's hand.'

'Yet another of my skills. I have an excellent eye and ability with a pen, a passable imitation of any hand is child's play for me. After all, the letter I brought with me in order to win your trust easily deceived you.'

'The letter from my father?'

'Yes. But certain additions were penned by myself. I am sure he would have expressed those sentiments had he been able. It makes little difference.'

To Nerissa it made all the difference in the world. Her throat tightened with nausea. She had wept over that letter, imagined it being penned with a loving weakened hand. And it had been a fake.

'I did however care for your father in his last illness. That was true. No-one else would go near him, fearing contagion — once Brook had succumbed also. Although I have to admit, Brook's illness was contrived by myself.

Bribery, poison, easily achieved where life and loyalty are cheap. Do not look so horrified, I did not kill him, did I? Although if I had realised what a nuisance he would become, I would have made a more complete work of it. Be thankful, without my forbearance, you would never have experienced the great love that you hold for each other. Regretfully shortlived but no doubt worthwhile.'

'Shortlived? What do you mean? We will never stop loving each other.'

'I learn from my mistakes.' There was something in the way he spoke that chilled her more than anything else he had said. He stood up. 'So Miss Cleveland, I take my leave.' She saw that he was holding the key in his hand and knew what he meant to do. 'You are not going to abandon us here?'

He laughed. 'Yes.'

'Not with the door locked?'

'There would be little point in leaving it open. You would have your fine friend from the British Museum, if indeed he is, after me in a moment.'

'But we may never be discovered.' Nerissa tried to keep her voice clear and calm. She had to convince him.

'A just repayment for the slights I have suffered. From his lordship in particular. I have noted every one, I assure you. As you have elected to throw in your lot with him, though with very poor taste, you must share his fate. Regrettable,' he shrugged, 'but necessary.' He turned towards the door. She must stop him. But how?

He turned back. She thought at first, her heart leaping, that he had changed his mind. But his malicious smile proved he had not. 'At least you will be together. For all time. How many loving couples can claim as much?'

10

'You cannot do this,' Nerissa said in a low voice, while her mind tested and rejected various possibilities. What could she make use of within the chamber? There were several small statuettes that Martin had left behind. On a ledge to her right was a dog-headed figure. It might be within her reach if Martin could be distracted.

By the door was a strong leather bag, no doubt containing the stone and her father's notes. She knew the size of the missing pieces and the Rosetta Stone was black basalt. The bag would be heavy. He would not lift it easily. He would have to turn away from her to pick it up. She said, 'Take anything you like, but please spare us. We will not send a pursuit after you, I promise you.'

'It makes no difference. I am taking

what I want. You have nothing left to bargain with.'

'Our deaths will be on your conscience.' Now. She would have one chance only.

'I think I can deal with that.' He laughed and bent to take hold of the bag's handles.

Nerissa took a deep breath, seized the dog by the neck and hurled both herself and the figure at Martin's bent head.

At the same time, there was a flurry of movement from the floor and Lord Brook also launched himself forward. Instead of reaching their target, they collided with each other as Martin stepped back. He only needed to swing the bag at them, laughing as he did so and Nerissa felt herself tumbling sideways, out of the stone tomb and into Lord Brook. They fell together, limbs hopelessly entangled.

'A brave attempt,' Martin sneered. 'And now I must take my leave.'

'Wait,' Lord Brook shouted. 'Let her go. Take your revenge on me if you must but spare Nerissa. She has done nothing to deserve this.'

'Has she not? Perhaps in the time remaining, she may reflect on the unwisdom of rejecting me. Making me look a fool.' The door opened on to the outside air, they were so near, before Martin slammed it behind him. The candle blew out in the draught.

Nerissa could hardly breathe from the impact of the fall. She fought against a wave of panic before a long cold breath entered her lungs. But what about Brook? 'Are you all right?' Her fingers found his face.

He groaned. 'I saved all my strength for that one chance. I failed you. Are you hurt?'

'No. As long as you are alive, that is all I ask.' Lying on the cold ground with his arms around her, for the moment nothing else mattered. Together they could achieve anything.

Lord Brook said, 'I should have told you everything from the first. All my suspicions.'

‘I was stubborn too. If you had warned me against him, I would not have listened.’

‘And I was jealous of your obvious fondness for him. At first because I arrogantly thought you were mine by right. But I very soon began to love the woman you had become for yourself.’

‘There was so much I missed. Was Martin right? Is Mr Northcott from the British Museum?’

‘No. As I told you, I knew him from my schooldays but he is now based at the Horse Guards’, the QuarterMaster General’s Department. When I first considered a French involvement, I called upon Northcott. His department is entrusted with secret work against the French.’

His hand caressed her shoulder. ‘I know this is safe with you. But then in the end, Martin was too clever for us. We underestimated him. And now, my love, if you feel you might stand, I think we must try to relight the candle.’

Nerissa realised he had been talking

to allow her time to recover. 'I'll try.' The confined space was now an advantage as gingerly they pulled themselves to their feet.

'There is a tinder box to the right of the door,' Lord Brook said. 'I saw Martin use it after he carried you in.'

Once they had light, the situation seemed more hopeful. 'There,' Lord Brook said with triumph. 'And now we must see about getting out of here.' He was still pale and with dried blood smeared across his face but he was grinning.

'There is another room,' Nerissa said, with a confidence she did not feel. 'I even tried to tell him because there may well be further antiquities of value inside. I would have sacrificed everything in exchange for your life. But he would not listen.'

'And no need,' said Lord Brook cheerfully, 'because here I am alive and well and we shall get out of this somehow. I swear it. If there is another room, there may well be a way out.'

'Yes.' Nerissa had never heard of one but it was possible. As children, they had never been allowed to play or search in here. She had only accompanied her parents as a particular treat. Since her mother's death, Giles Cleveland had kept the Grotto in memory of his wife. Thus it had provided the perfect hiding place for the missing portion of the stone. Or so he must have thought.

She would have to come to terms with what he had done and try to understand. Surely as soon as he had solved the puzzle of the stone, he would have revealed his discovery to the world?

And now Martin had come here to despoil and pillage the place most dear to her . . . and all to serve France. She tried to distract herself. There was something else Martin had said which she did not understand. 'What did Martin mean when he said Sophie had other concerns? Something about her beloved not arriving at the assembly?'

'Ah, yes. Sophie is secretly engaged to a naval lieutenant, the younger son of a good family. He is expected home shortly; Sophie had word that he would attend the assembly but he did not arrive. And now we know why.' He frowned. 'That was sheer cruelty and mischief-making on Martin's part. But he will be here soon, however, and I intend to speak up for him to her parents now I am returned. Do not worry, their happiness is assured.'

Nerissa said, more lightly than she felt, 'And if you are to persuade her parents, we must first get out of here.'

'There is no doubt about that,' Lord Brook said cheerfully. 'Even if we do not succeed in making our escape immediately, I am certain Northcott will not be long deceived by Martin's forged note. He is very sharp.'

She knew he was trying to keep her spirits up. 'Yes,' she said with a smile. 'But there is no harm in searching for a way out while we wait. It will keep us warm. And to begin, I will show you the other room.' If the mechanisms still worked, without the benefit of her father's constant attention. Don't think of that. Or that they might well be searching for an escape route that had long fallen into dis-use.

Martin had taken the best of the statues and three niches in this first chamber now stood empty. The gods of good fortune were missing, she thought wryly, but there were two remaining. Her would-be weapon, another with the head of a jackal and a female figure. If Martin had tried to lift them, he would have found them seemingly too solid to remove. Fortunate that he had not approached them in the right way.

She wiped her damp hands on the muslin of her skirt to improve her grip, one more stain would make little difference now, and closed her eyes, trying to remember. Her father had manipulated the statues so swiftly. And some of her grandfather's mechanisms responded badly to a mistake — a trap for any intruder.

Lord Brook waited silently, not seeking to hurry her.

Nerissa took a quick breath, grasped the jackal's head and twisted it to the right. Her heart had surely stopped beating. Would it work? Had she chosen the wrong order? No, she heard a reassuring click and knew she had only seconds in which to turn the other to the left. Yes, thank goodness, that too clicked into place and the wall bearing the female goddess swung away.

'Well done.' Lord Brook's voice was jubilant. 'Wait, I'll get the candle.' They entered the room hand in hand. Lord Brook gasped. 'The best of all. Giles hinted as much to me but I had no idea.'

In the light of the flickering candle flame, the room gleamed with gold — boxes, panels, and small items of furniture. And holding court over all the riches sat a painted and jewelled statue of a woman.

'Isis,' Nerissa said, 'holding the infant Horus.' Her eyes misted. 'My parents arranged this room together.' She tried to keep her voice even. 'They were so secure in their love for each other and they were to be parted so soon.'

'A love like theirs can never be destroyed,' Lord Brook said softly. 'No matter how long the separation. And now they are together for all time.'

She smiled at him. 'It may seem fanciful but I feel so close to them here. Maybe they are giving our love their blessing.' She thought, if we can only get out of here and bit back a sob.

Lord Brook set the candle down and drew her towards him. As they kissed, a warmth and intensity she had never known swept through her, giving her the strength and courage to carry on. As he must have known it would.

But how much time did they have before Martin's candle died? There were so many protuberances and seeming levers in this room to be pulled, pushed and twisted.

'We must begin,' Lord Brook said stoutly. 'Do we have to act in any particular order?'

Nerissa put a hand to her forehead. 'Let me think a moment. By trying everything indiscriminately, we may damage the workings. And I believe that anything too obvious may be discounted.'

She drew near to the goddess who smiled upon them serenely, looking beyond them. Nerissa found herself following the gaze and turning to the wall behind her, as if to see what Isis might be looking at. The walls were painted in accurate imitation of an Egyptian tomb. A variety of gods and goddesses stood in solemn procession.

'Apuat,' Lord Brook said suddenly, recognising one. 'Surely? The opener of the ways.'

'Yes, and that must mean . . . '

'That there is indeed a way out.'

Nerissa felt fearful with relief. But there was no time for weakness. Already the candle was three quarters gone. She turned back to look at Isis. There was something about her that did not seem quite right, if she could only work it out.

Brook did not hurry her although he too must have been conscious of time flickering by. She regarded the goddess carefully. Every detail seemed correct and she had seen many statues and paintings to compare. But wait, perhaps it was not the statue itself?

She leaned forward, peering at the pendant the goddess wore. Why had she not realised? It was an almost exact replica of hers. But the puzzle shapes that had become the key were not quite the same. There was something else, small but easily recognisable to the knowledgeable eye. Apuat again.

She touched the small figure with gentle fingers, not wishing to disturb anything too soon. 'This figure has been fashioned as part of the statue. In fact, I do not believe that this statue was ever brought from Egypt. Like my pendant, it has been made here.' She spoke softly as if to herself. 'Which way to turn it? We cannot afford to make a mistake.'

'The figure is facing the opposite way on the wall painting,' Brook said. 'Is that a pointer?'

'Yes, you are right. I believe it must be. Well, we shall have to try it.' She grasped the figure with the familiar technique she had used in the outer chamber. To her surprise, it moved easily, almost as if oiled but there was no time to query that. Beyond the statue another portion of painted panelling slid aside. Inviting, and yet, Supposing the passage-way led only to another hidden room, containing yet more riches? Wealth that would be of no use to them if they could not escape.

'Come then,' Lord Brook said.

'Yes.' Nerissa stepped forward bravely, trying to think where the tunnel might lead or how far they might be walking beneath the hill. Was the passage sloping downwards? If so, they might be going far underground with no way of retracing their steps.

The walls were at first merely damp and then water was dripping from the stones. Droplets of mud splashed on to her feet and ankles. She could only see the dim circle of decreasing light behind them and no idea of what lay before them. She peered forwards into the darkness.

The candle spluttered, flared briefly and went out. Nerissa fought back a gasp that might all too easily have become a scream.

'It's all right,' Lord Brook said. 'We could not have found the passage without the candle but now all we have to do is follow the walls, we can feel our way.'

That last kiss, Nerissa thought. They had wasted precious time with the candle still glowing. Were they to die here because of those kisses? But at least there need be no such holding back now. Lord Brook's arms were round her. 'Courage, my love,' he whispered.

'I love you.'

'And I you. And we are together. Alone, this hardship might overwhelm either of us. But together we can achieve anything.'

They must. Unthinkable that they might not survive. Brook was right. They would come through this. They began to move forward, feeling each step with care. And to Nerissa's surprise, they had moved less than twenty paces before her hands could go no further. There was some kind of solid barrier before them. A dead end? Another of her grandfather's tricks?

Beside her, Brook was moving his hands over the surface. 'No, it's all right. It's a door.'

'With a keyhole,' Nerissa cried. 'And a handle.'

'So once again we need a key,' Lord Brook said cheerfully.

Not another puzzle, Nerissa thought desperately. Must they go back through the passage to the inner room in search of another key? Impossible in the dark. She scrabbled around the door hopelessly and found a narrow ledge. 'Wait, there is something here.' She could not quite reach.

Lord Brook's hands followed hers

and reached upwards. 'It's here. We have it.' As if her grandfather had tired at last of his puzzles and taken pity on anyone who had struggled this far. Brook was already inserting the key in the lock. 'If it will only turn . . . '

But would it? The walls were so wet and the whole atmosphere chilly with damp. 'I know,' Nerissa said. They could not give up now when they were so near. She began to make her way back. No more than twenty paces, surely, since they had been plunged into the dark? She counted as she walked, feeling the floor with frantic hands and feet. And yes, it was here, where she had dropped it, lying in a welcome puddle of warm candle grease. She called, 'Perhaps this will ease the key.'

'Of course. The exact thing.' She could hear the warmth in his voice. They worked well together, reaching out into the dark to bring the key to the grease, their fingers hardly stumbling. And at last Lord Brook found the keyhole once more and yes, the key turned smoothly. Lord Brook grasped the handle and with a groaning of hinges, the door jarred open.

11

The rush of air was blissfully cold and there was the tumultuous sound of water falling on rock. 'I know where we are,' Nerissa cried. They stood inside a small dim cave, in what seemed like the brightest daylight after the darkness they had encountered. 'I often used to come here.'

'You never brought me. I had no idea it was here.'

'It was my special, secret place. But I had no idea there was a door.' She turned to examine how the solid door had been skilfully fashioned to resemble the rock. Even the keyhole was hidden from this side, disguised as a crack between two stones.

'So all is well,' Lord Brook said. 'We are safe.'

Nerissa hesitated. 'Well . . . '

'If you came here as a child . . . '

'That was years ago. We are standing behind the waterfall. However, I am certain it must still be possible. There were always plenty of footholds and I am taller now which will make it easier.' Hand in hand, they clambered out over the fallen slabs and pebbles to gaze out at their surroundings. 'Not as bad as I feared,' Nerissa said brightly. 'From below, looking at the waterfall, I thought it was impassable. And after the quarrel, I did not have the heart to come here. But see, it is almost a staircase.'

'You must stay here,' Lord Brook said. 'I will not have you risking your neck. And I will go and seek help.'

'No. No further partings. We go together.' She glared at him.

Brook laughed. 'Do not look so fierce. Thinking about it, I would be foolish to leave you here alone when we do not know how far ahead Martin might be.'

'He has gone, surely? He has all that he came for — and more.'

'I'm sure he has. But I have no intention of taking that risk. And I am not going to pretend that the danger does not exist. We have been through too much together for pretence.'

Nerissa nodded. Martin had been her least consideration, but now Lord Brook had voiced his concern, she realised she had a feeling, an instinct, that Martin might not be so far away after all. 'But the sooner we begin, the better.' She knew she sounded braver than she felt. One slip on the wet rock and there would be a heavy fall to the stream below.

It was not as difficult, however, as she had feared. Two steps down and they were leaving the spray; her way led outwards and downwards at the same time and the footholds were just as she remembered. Her hands also went straight to the places she recalled. Not quite as easy as when she had skipped up and down without thought, or so it seemed, as a child. But better than she had feared all the same.

An anxious moment when one of the ledges gave way under Lord Brook's weight but he kicked out before finding a useful crevice and righted himself. In moments his hands had found another hold and he was down and past the danger. It could only have been several minutes before they were both on firm ground but it had seemed like an age.

Only then did Nerissa realise how badly her legs were shaking and that her dress and stockings were black with mud. There was no time to rest here however. She thrust her weariness away and said briskly, 'We must walk along the stream, I'm afraid, though as the gorge becomes more shallow, there is a path of sorts. And beyond the Leap and the stone seat, there are steps returning to the wood. From then on, the walk has been prettified and made suitable for ladies.'

'How very tame that must seem to you,' Lord Brook said, grinning.

'After today I shall be more than content to admire our waterfall from a distance.' She knew he must be as weary as she was and that if her head was aching from the injuries received from Martin, his must be worse. But neither made any complaint. She said, 'Soon we shall be in sight of the Leap and the rest will be easy.'

'I remember, once at the Leap, we are back to the stream's original course. I am familiar with all this. Wait.' He tilted his head, listening, 'Let me go first now.'

'What is it?' But already Lord Brook was edging past her and now she too could hear voices ahead. He turned to her with a finger to his lips, gesturing that she should go no further. But if there was yet more danger ahead, Nerissa intended to see it for herself. She ignored him and followed.

When he stopped suddenly, she almost cannoned into him. They peered round the bend in the stream before the Leap and she took a deep breath of relief, recognising the several figures there — Northcott, Cobham, young

Jack and two of Lord Brook's men with a trestle. Moving awkwardly as they worked to free something from the stream.

Lord Brook said, 'It's Martin.'

Northcott had been suspicious of the note from the first, he told them. Instigating a search of the grounds, he had seen Martin taking a horse and riding off at speed. Northcott had given chase, trying to head him off and Martin had recklessly attempted the Leap and failed.

There was no sign of the pieces of the Rosetta Stone. Somehow they had fallen from the bag and merged with the stones and pebbles in the swift flowing stream. 'We could search for a year and never find it.' Lord Brook said regretfully. 'These papers were still in Martin's bag. But I'm afraid they were unreadable.'

'This quest has caused enough suffering,' Nerissa said quietly. 'I am sure the puzzle will be solved sooner or later.' She regretted the loss of her father's work but even more keenly did she feel the absence of the small figures on her pendant.

* * *

A day's rest saw both Nerissa and Lord Brook fully recovered. The following morning, Nerissa dressed quickly, half thinking that Lady Hartness might come in to insist upon a further day in bed, when all she wanted was to be with her dear Edward.

She smiled, remembering her joy of the previous morning. And how she had been filled with happiness and eager to see Lord Brook again knowing that they loved each other. But she had come down to a nightmare, with Brook already unconscious and imprisoned. She would never recover her precious pendant but she had so much to be thankful for.

Lord Brook came out of the breakfast room and his smile told her everything. His happiness was no less than hers. He held out his arms and she stepped joyfully towards him, only to be halted by a discreet cough. Wilkins was frowning a little as he came forwards from the corridor leading to the steward's room. 'I am sorry to disturb you, but Jack Bartlett was asking for you. He is most insistent and has been hanging around for an hour at least. But at a word from you, Miss, I will send him packing. In your delicate state of health . . . '

'Of course I will see him,' Nerissa smiled. She went at once to the steward's room where Jack was waiting. 'I have something for you, Miss — I found it downstream.'

'Oh, Jack — my pendant! Thank you so much. You have no idea how much it means to me.'

'I think I do, Miss. Your father was a great man. It's only right that this should come back to you.'

Lord Brook took it gently. 'It is hardly damaged. We may easily have it repaired.'

'And Miss, there is something else.' The boy had a troubled look. 'I know that the secret came out, but I need to tell you that it was none of my doing. Mr Martin got into the Grotto on his own.'

'We know that, but how could it be your doing?'

'Ah . . . ' Lord Brook said, placing a hand on her arm. 'I believe I understand.'

'I never told.' Jack was twisting his cap in his hands. 'The old master entrusted the Grotto's secrets to my father. It was his job to see all the workings. But he was sworn never to tell of it.'

The oil, Nerissa thought. The way the mechanisms had opened so easily . . .

'He was to say nothing.' Jack was speaking with eyes half closed as if reciting a lesson. 'Not until Mr Giles, your father, Miss, approached him. That was to be the way of it. That would mean that Mr Giles had unravelled the puzzle, you see. Because the old master was a great one for puzzles.'

Brook and Nerissa exchanged a smiling glance. 'We know.'

'And before he died, my dad passed the secrets on to me. Assuring me that when Mr Giles died, you would approach me in your turn. And until you did so, I wasn't to speak of it to anyone. When you said nothing, I wasn't sure what to do. And I didn't like the way that Mr Martin kept creeping around, and Mr Northcott and Lord Brook too. So I resolved to keep my word and say nothing until all the strangers had gone and keep on with my duties in secret as best I could.'

'And you did well,' Nerissa said warmly. 'Without your care, we would not have escaped.'

'Be assured, Jack, there will always be a place for you here,' Brook said. 'We are in your debt.'

'So that is another mystery solved,' Nerissa said, as the boy left the room.

'And not the only one,' Lord Brook said. 'You remember the scrap of paper I brought with me? That your father had tried to write?'

'As if I would forget. '*N, there is danger — ask B*'.' Her eyes lit up as she worked it out. 'Of course. I took B to mean either Bernard Martin or yourself. Which only added to my confusion. But maybe your father was sending me to Jack Bartlett.' She sighed. 'If only he had found the strength to finish the note.'

'No matter,' Lord Brook said softly. 'We have found our way through the maze, one way or another. And I think your father and grandfather would have approved of our efforts.' He stepped closer, still holding the pendant in one hand. 'The clasp is still intact. May I replace it for you, where it belongs?'

She nodded, hardly breathing and turned while Lord Brook's skilful hands brushed the back of her neck. 'You are taking a very long time about it, my lord.'

'The clasp is a little loose. I believe you will need my assistance with it from now on.' He stroked the back of her neck. 'I suggest we put the troubled memories of the last few days behind us and only recall the sweetest moment of my life. One that will stay with me forever.'

Nerissa smiled. 'That evening at the assembly. I will never forget. It seems so long ago and yet no time at all.' She turned to face him. 'I knew then that you loved me. I shall never part with this pendant. It brought us together.' She laughed suddenly. 'I do not believe the fastening was loose at all. This was just an excuse.'

'I need no excuse to kiss you,' Lord Brook said.

'Or I you,' Nerissa whispered. 'For the rest of our lives.'

And Lady Hartness, seeking to enter the room, stepped discreetly away with a smile of the deepest satisfaction.